It was his first ride down the Cannonball Chute. With heart pounding expectantly, he stared into the darkness of the tunnel before pushing off with his hands. The shock of the cold water rushed over his face. He sped down the tube, twisting, turning, looping. It was pitch black and the taste of chlorine filled his mouth. The tunnel echoed with the pounding of water and someone screamed. Or was that him? He zoomed faster, faster, faster, hurtling on around the curves and twists of the water slide.

Then nothing.

No water, no pool. Just a rush of air and the sensation of dropping a great distance, his stomach left behind. With a tremendous wallop he hit the water and sank.

He opened his eyes. Slowly a hot panic crept through his insides. Where on earth was he?

Jo Coghlan was a primary school teacher and administrator before embarking on a writing career. *Switched* is her first children's novel. Jo lives in Perth, Western Australia.

SWITCHED

Jo Coghlan

Fremantle Arts Centre Press

Australia's finest small publisher

For
my son James and his friend Ben
who were there when Garry's adventure began,
husband Peter, parents Mardi and Jim,
and parents-in-law Connie and Phil.

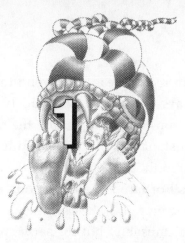

Gasping for breath, Garry surfaced, his lungs at bursting point. He struggled to a low wall and hauled himself up, flicking water from his hair, trying to calm his breathing, coughing up water. What had happened? In a daze he looked around.

He was sitting on the edge of a deep pool. It was strangely quiet. There was no laughter, no kids splashing in shallow pools and no mums sipping cappuccinos at shaded tables. Garry shivered. Where was he? What had happened to Aqua Mania? He shook his head and closed his eyes, recalling the previous couple of minutes.

He had been standing in a queue at the top of the Cannonball Chute, the water slide at Aqua Mania. It was his twelfth birthday and he was celebrating with his friend, Cameron. Way down below was his mum, relaxing under her multicoloured umbrella.

Up there was like being on the top of the world and everything seemed so small. A hotchpotch of

5

suburban roofs spread far beyond the fun park, and shiny cars on the coastal road twinkling in the brilliant sunshine. To the right, the river meandered to the distant city of Port Vlamingh and the hills beyond. To the left, pockets of pine trees and sandy beaches bordered the enormous expanse of the Indian Ocean.

It was unusually hot for early spring and Garry was relieved when Cameron finally disappeared down the slide and it was his turn. This was his first ride down the Cannonball Chute. With heart pounding expectantly, he waited for the lifeguard to give him the all clear. Positioning himself on the mat, he stared into the darkness of the tunnel before pushing off with his hands. The shock of the cold water rushed over his face. He sped down the tube, twisting, turning, looping, all the while hanging on tightly to the handles of the mat. It was pitch black and the taste of chlorine filled his mouth. The tunnel echoed with the pounding of water and someone screamed. Or was that *him*? He zoomed faster, faster, faster, hurtling on around the curves and twists of the water slide.

Then a pinprick of light was rushing towards him. He'd come to the straight part, the cannon, and with a thrill he anticipated crashing into the shallow pool below.

Suddenly, the mat slipped out from under his body and his chest was being bombarded with what felt like a million tickling fingers. He just managed to register that it felt oddly pleasant, as though he was floating, when he shot into the flash of blinding light. Instinctively, he closed his eyes against the wall of water and sunlight.

Then nothing.

No water, no pool. Just a rush of air and the sensation of dropping a great distance, his stomach left behind. With a tremendous wallop he hit the water and sank.

Garry opened his eyes. He was sitting on the edge of a strange pool, shivering with cold and shock. He had no idea where he was.

He looked for Cameron who had come down the water slide before him. The slide! Looking up he saw a gigantic snake-like water slide, enclosed but completely transparent. This was not the Cannonball Chute but he had definitely fallen out of it!

Slowly a hot panic crept through his insides. Where on earth was he? Wherever it was, he was no longer alone. A big man appeared on the other side of the pool and started shouting. Garry couldn't make out what he was saying.

Then he was startled by a noise above him and he looked up to see a boy coming down the transparent slide at an incredible speed. The kid shot out of the end of the tunnel, somersaulted twice and dived perfectly into the pool.

'Nice one! What a dive!'

Garry whipped around to see two girls sitting behind him. The boy waved to them and swam to the edge of the pool. Effortlessly, he heaved himself out of the water and joined them.

'Rorgan Tyne!' It was the man yelling again. 'Nice that you've finally joined us,' he bellowed sarcastically. 'Where have you been? Never mind — I don't want to know. Stop mucking about and get back up there. Rorgan Tyne, are you listening to me?'

Garry looked across the pool at the tall, stern-faced man striding towards him. He wondered who this Rorgan Tyne was but his mind was confused, still trying to make sense of his surroundings. Maybe he'd hit his head on the way down. Maybe if he closed his eyes and blocked his ears for a while all this would go away. Eyes shut, he put two fingers in his ears and started counting to twenty.

'*Rorgan Tyne!*'

Garry's whole body sprang to attention. His skin itched all over. It seemed too tight, unfamiliar, as though it belonged to someone else. The man now stood over him, arms folded. His bushy moustache partly obscured his upper lip.

'That's it, Rorgan Tyne. I've just about had enough. You muck around in training, you disobey me, you pretend you can't hear me. I'm running out of patience.'

Garry stared. The man was yelling at *him*!

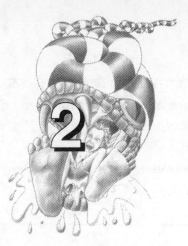

'But I'm not Rorg Thingamy, whatever you said. I'm Garry Tenon.' His voice quavered. It was all starting to get too much and he felt dizzy and his skin itched like crazy. *Where was Cameron? What was happening?*

'Stop fooling around!' shouted the man and then he waved in the direction of the water slide and whispered menacingly, 'Get back up there and dive properly. This is your last chance, Rorgan Tyne. Otherwise, you're off the team. I don't care who your father is!'

Turning to the three kids behind him he growled, 'One more dive each. And for goodness sake, Pree Stappa, put that mat in the storeroom!'

'Yes, Trainer,' the kids mumbled. A short athletic-looking girl with a cascade of freckles across her nose and cheeks picked up Garry's mat and hurried off with the other two kids towards a tower on the other side of the pool.

Garry ran after them, his brain pounding with

confusion. Perhaps the kids could tell him what the hell was going on. They entered a lift at the base of the tower and he stood silently, bewildered, as the lift ascended. His thoughts were interrupted by the freckle-faced girl.

'Why do you do that to Trainer, Rorgan Tyne?' she asked, running her hand through her cropped sandy hair and looking straight at Garry.

'But I'm *not* Rorgan Tyne!' cried Garry.

The girl rolled her eyes upwards and the other kids groaned.

'I don't understand you,' she continued. 'You're one of our best divers but you mess up all the time. If you get kicked off the team, we'll never win.'

'Yeah, Rorgan Tyne,' said the tall boy beside her. 'You might think you're very funny but I think you're selfish and dumb.' The other girl nodded in agreement.

This was too much! He had never been accused of 'messing up' or of being selfish or dumb. He was a regular kid who liked fooling around with his friends but he didn't 'muck up' and he wasn't dumb. He was actually pretty smart and worked hard at school.

What was Freckle-Face on about? What 'team' was he on and what did they have to win? He couldn't be *that* good at diving. He'd never dived before in his life. Questions ricocheted in his brain.

'Look, I don't know you. I don't even know where I am. Why do you keep calling me Rorgan Tyne?'

But his voice was drowned out by the lift jolting to a stop and the doors opening. The kids shuffled out and stood in front of the entrance to the slide. The thing twisted and curled like a snake on its downward journey to the pool far, far below.

Garry's stomach lurched. *Man oh man! This baby is big!*

Freckle-Face looked at him strangely.

'Hey, *now* what's the matter, Rorgan Tyne?' she asked.

Momentarily Garry forgot his amazement and turned angrily towards her.

'Stop calling me Rorgan Tyne, you idiot. My name's Garry. I bet I don't even look like this Rorgan Tyne.'

'Oh yeah?' She took Garry by the shoulders and twirled him around so he faced the mirrored doors of the lift. 'Then who's that?'

Garry froze. The reflection that stared back at him with piercing black eyes was not his.

Garry was shocked. His mouth fell open in disbelief and he gave a strangled cry. Where was his blond curly hair? His brown eyes? What had happened to the braces on his teeth? He touched the wet hair and the unfamiliar contours of his face. His finger traced a scar on his chin. The reflection in the mirror did the same. Stretching his fingers, he inspected his hands. No wonder his skin felt strange. It belonged to someone else — this Rorgan Tyne — the face in the mirror he recognised — had seen it recently — but where? He looked back at his reflection and his heart pounded with panic.

'Drey Allenbow,' said a voice behind him, 'you're first, then Marsimony Brin, Pree Stappa and then Rorgan Tyne.'

Garry swung around. A tall muscular woman smiled at the kids.

'Squeeze your legs into your body, children,' she

continued, 'and throw your arms down quickly after the somersault.'

'Yes, Mother,' said the kids.

'And you're all over-rotating. Keep your eyes on your entry spot in the water.'

'Yes, Mother,' they repeated.

'Right, Drey Allenbow, off you go.'

The boy lay on his stomach and pushed off through the entrance of the huge slide. Garry watched his journey downwards. Like a rocket he shot out of the tunnel and into the air, somersaulted and dived with barely a splash. He scooped gracefully under water and reappeared at the side of the pool. Gulping, Garry watched Marsimony Brin and the freckled one, Pree Stappa, do their dives. He turned to face his reflection again. Where had he seen this boy? How could he possibly have become him?

'Ah, Rorgan Tyne. Come here, love,' cooed Mother as Pree Stappa finished her dive. Garry stepped forward. His heart beat faster. It was his turn. 'Now look, please stop all this nonsense. Trainer is very cross with you and you'll be off the team if you don't change your attitude.'

She spoke gently but sternly as she looked into Garry's eyes. He just nodded, wondering how on earth he was going to *survive* this humungous slide, let alone *dive* out of it. The Cannonball Chute was one thing — but this?

'Remember, Rorgan Tyne,' continued the woman whispering into Garry's ear. 'You're the best we've got, love. Don't spoil your chances, all right?'

Again Garry nodded. He was incredibly confused; things were happening too fast. One minute he was Garry, celebrating his birthday at Aqua Mania, and the next he was Rorgan Tyne, some strange guy with attitude — someone he'd seen somewhere before — a brilliant diver but a complete nerd who fooled around in class. How was he, Garry Who Looked Like Rorgan Tyne, supposed to act? Then there was 'Trainer' and these kids with funny names and now 'Mother'. Who were they?

And this slide and dive thing. It looked difficult. It looked dangerous. All he knew was he had to somersault and then dive into the water. That's all he had to do! Oh yeah, sure!

'Rorgan Tyne,' prompted Mother, smiling kindly, 'are you listening? Keep your legs straight and you'll go faster.'

You'll go faster. He looked up sharply. Someone had said those exact words to him just a few moments ago. Someone on the Cannonball Chute. A boy. And then he remembered.

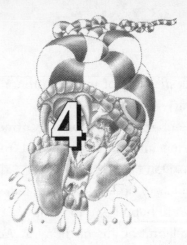

He had only seen the boy briefly. He was behind him in the queue. Kids were jostling one another and suddenly Garry was pushed forwards, his mat torpedoing out of his hands. The kid behind him handed it back and said good-naturedly, 'I think you might need this. You'll go faster.'

He remembered the boy's black eyes, slim build, faint scar on his chin and straight, white teeth. He had tanned, smooth skin, and on his wrist, a black leather strap covering a watch.

That was it. A brief conversation. And somehow he had become that boy!

Garry's heart thumped wildly. This must be a crazy mistake. Yes, that was it. It was a mistake or a dream or something. He'd go down this slide and find himself back in the fun park. Yes! He breathed more easily and shut his eyes trying to envisage the city of Port Vlamingh from the top of the Cannonball Chute at Aqua Mania.

'Rorgan Tyne? Are you ready?' Mother pointed to the slide.

'Yes,' replied Garry. He lay down awkwardly on his stomach and the warm water lapped around his body. He gazed into the see-through tunnel then looked back to the woman and waited for further instructions, but all she said was, 'Off you go then.'

So this was it. Goodbye Rorgan Tyne. Hello Garry. He pushed off with his hands and the journey began.

Down, down he went through the twists and turns of the gigantic slide, the water roaring in his ears. This was fantastic! Way better than the Cannonball Chute. And there was no mat. Just a smooth sheet of water carrying him swiftly around the loops and corners. It was as though the water was suspended in air just above the floor of the tunnel. Every twist brought a thrilling sensation. But most extraordinary was the feeling of being tickled by invisible fingers. Then he saw the end of the tunnel and his body tensed, ready to hit the water, the shallow water of the pool at the fun park.

'Please! Please! Please!' he yelled as he shot through the mouth of the tunnel.

He thrust out his arms to meet the water. But there was no water. Instead he felt an unexpected rush of elation as the force of his journey pushed him forwards, spinning into sideways twists through the air. Dizzily, he saw water rushing up to meet him and a blur of faces and colour sliding past. At the last second he instinctively stretched out his arms in a dive and then all he heard were the muffled sounds of an underwater world.

He surfaced, swam to the side of the pool and heaved himself out, coughing up water. His heart thumped and the elation seeped away. In the distance he heard clapping and cheering. He took no notice. He was still in this strange world and he felt miserable.

'Rorgan Tyne!'

It was Trainer hurrying across to him. Garry, head down, clutched his knees to his chest as he sat at the edge of the pool. He waited for Trainer's anger. Hot tears at the back of his eyes threatened to spill out any second.

'I knew you could do it!' cried Trainer, moustache twitching with excitement.

What? Garry looked up. Trainer was smiling! Smiling!

'Rorgan Tyne, that was brilliant! I knew that one day you'd do a triple twist torpedo just like the Great Lado Kaan!'

'Thanks but I don't know ...' began Garry, standing up and taking the towel Trainer offered him. He looked at the other three standing silently next to him and caught Pree Stappa's puzzled expression. She seemed to be studying him.

'That was sensational! Sensational!' beamed Trainer again. 'We can use that in the competition. We can't lose now. Okay, everyone, that's enough for today. Off you go home. See you tomorrow. Plenty of rest now, and especially you, Rorgan Tyne.'

'Yes, Trainer,' mumbled Garry and then he cupped his hand over his mouth. *What was he saying?*

Garry watched the three kids saunter off. He desperately wanted to go home, to *his* home. He had no idea about Rorgan Tyne's home. Would Rorgan Tyne's mum — a completely different mum, someone Garry had never seen before — come and collect him and take him home? Home to a place he'd never set eyes on? Did Rorgan Tyne have a dad, brothers, sisters?

'Come on!' Pree Stappa called, turning to Garry.

The other kids stopped.

'What's the matter?' sneered Drey Allenbow, tossing his towel casually over his shoulder. 'Think you're too good to walk with us now?'

'Leave him alone,' said Marsimony Brin. She flicked her wet ponytail from side to side. 'You're just jealous because he can dive better than you can.'

'I'm not jealous,' the tall boy retorted. 'Wonder boy here might have jagged a good dive but he'll

20

never be able to do it again. Tomorrow he'll be fooling round again, I bet.'

Pree Stappa said nothing. She gave Garry a long searching look as though trying to figure something out.

Before he could say anything, the woman they called 'Mother' bustled up behind him and ushered the children through a gate that separated the swimming complex from a large two-storey house.

'Well done, children. Wonderful dive, Rorgan Tyne,' she said, nodding her head in approval as she pushed open the back door. 'You must all be starving! Showers first, then an early dinner. And please don't leave your towel on the floor, Marsimony Brin,' she smiled at the girl with the ponytail.

Garry studied her. Was she the kids' real mum? Were the kids brothers and sisters? They didn't *look* alike.

Wearily, he followed the other three through a kitchen and a dining room and then upstairs. He was hungry and exhausted. He figured that all he had to do was be himself. Sooner or later they'd all realise he wasn't Rorgan Tyne and then maybe they'd help him. Maybe.

Upstairs, Garry cautiously opened the door that warned: RORGAN TYNE'S ROOM. KEEP OUT! It was like a bombsite. Clothes littered the floor and

21

escaped from cupboards and drawers. Beneath the mess were glimpses of a desk, an unmade bed and a faded carpet. Garry headed for the bathroom off one side of the room.

After a long hot shower and dressed in fresh clothes he managed to find in the chaos, he felt better, even in his strange skin. Following the delicious smells of dinner cooking, he trudged downstairs to the dining room where Pree Stappa, Drey Allenbow and Marsimony Brin sat, heads together, whispering and peeling vegetables. As Garry appeared they stopped talking and stared at him. His stomach growled with hunger.

'Here,' said Pree Stappa pushing a chip packet towards him. 'Hungry?' She spoke as though issuing a challenge.

Garry nodded and eagerly hoed in. The three kids exchanged looks.

'That was a great dive today,' continued Pree Stappa. They all watched Garry.

'Thanks,' he said with his mouth full.

'Mother said to slice these up,' Marsimony Brin said, motioning to the carrots. She handed Garry a knife and cutting board. 'Want to help?'

'Thanks,' he said again, taking the knife and attacking the carrots.

Again they watched and exchanged glances. 'Who

taught you the triple twist torpedo?' This time it was Drey Allenbow who spoke.

Garry gave a tired sigh. 'Look, it was a fluke, okay? And while we're at it, I'm *not* Rorgan Tyne, you know.'

'We know you're not,' said Pree Stappa.

Garry stopped slicing and looked up.

'Man oh man! You *know*? But today you ...'

'Shh! Keep your voice down,' warned Drey Allenbow looking towards the kitchen. 'You *look* like Rorgan Tyne and you *sound* like him but you don't *act* like him.'

'Well I've been trying to tell ...'

'I thought you were fooling around,' Pree Stappa interrupted. 'Pretending not to be Rorgan Tyne. That's the sort of dumb thing he does. He keeps it up for hours. But then later on I knew for sure you weren't him. You had no idea what to do on the Snake today, did you?'

'The Snake?'

'The dive slide. We call it the Snake.'

'Well ... no ... I mean I've never ...'

'I know,' she said. 'You've never dived before, have you?'

Garry looked embarrassed. 'Was it *that* obvious?'

'Well it was to me. I mean you looked so scared and you kept watching everything we did as though

23

you really didn't know what to do. Rorgan Tyne is a good actor but not that good. And we know the triple twist torpedo was a fluke.'

'And by the way,' said Marsimony Brin, pointing to Garry's knife, 'Rorgan Tyne would never help. And he'd never say "thanks" or "please" or anything like that.'

'Sounds like a nice guy, this Rorgan Tyne,' laughed Garry, scratching his unfamiliar skin.

'And another thing,' said Marsimony Brin. 'Rorgan Tyne hates chips.'

'You're kidding! Poor guy! I love them!'

'I can see that!' she teased, holding the packet upside down. The last chips fell on the table. They all made a grab for them but Marsimony Brin was too fast.

Garry laughed. It wasn't so bad here, and now the kids knew he wasn't Rorgan Tyne, they'd help him.

'Where am I?' he asked.

'Lennox City,' replied Pree Stappa.

A sudden panic gripped him. He'd never *heard* of Lennox City. Where on earth was it? Was it *on* Earth? 'Look, I don't know how all this happened but I really want to go home. How do I get out of here?'

The kids looked at each other, puzzled.

'You haven't told us who you are,' Pree Stappa said quietly.

'My name's Garry Tenon.'

'How did you get here, Garry Tenon?'

'Just *Garry*, call me Garry.'

'All right, Garry. How did you get here?'

'I'm not sure,' he replied and then explained about Aqua Mania and how he'd seen the black-eyed boy. 'Then I went down the Cannonball Chute and here I am,' he concluded, rubbing the scar on his chin.

They listened, fascinated. Finally Pree Stappa said, 'So if you, Garry, became Rorgan Tyne, then Rorgan Tyne must have become …'

'Me!' exclaimed Garry. Why hadn't he thought of it before? Rorgan Tyne had become *him*! Maybe living in *his* house, with *his* family, using *his* things, hanging out with *his* friends.

'Pree Stappa!' It was the first time he'd said her name. 'What's going on? I want to go home! Tell me how to do it!'

Pree Stappa shook her head and said slowly, 'I don't know yet.'

'What don't you know?' It was Mother. She bustled into the room, swept the vegetables into a container and paused at the door on her way back to the kitchen.

The kids said nothing.

'Suit yourself,' she laughed. 'Come on, dinner's just about ready. We're eating in the kitchen tonight.'

'Please help me,' whispered Garry when Mother had gone.

'We'll talk later,' said Pree Stappa, standing up and moving towards the door.

The others followed and Garry trudged after them. He was suddenly tired again and not very hungry. He ate in silence and listened to the conversation, wondering about this world and how he could escape. It had to have something to do with the Snake. Strange how the kids didn't say anything to Mother about him; strange how Mother didn't realise he wasn't Rorgan Tyne. He ran his hand through his foreign stringy hair and yawned. He couldn't get used to this new body and he felt dizzy. Not surprising really, considering the day's events.

'You look tired,' said Mother as Garry yawned again. 'Big training day again tomorrow. I think you should get some sleep.'

'I think I will,' Garry said, pushing his plate away and standing up.

'See you later,' whispered Pree Stappa as he brushed passed her on his way upstairs. 'Your room, first thing tomorrow.'

'Yeah, yeah, whatever,' he said.

Sleep. That's what he needed. And tomorrow he'd wake up and everything would be normal again.

6

But it wasn't. Three faces swam in front of him.
Where had he seen them before? He had to get up.
School today. Monday. Sport. Great!

'Look, he's waking up,' said one of the faces.

Garry stretched and yawned, half asleep.

'Hey guys, you're still here,' he said dreamily.

'No, Garry,' said a familiar voice. '*You're* still here.'

Garry sat up on the bed, the events of the previous
day flashing through his mind. He raced to the mirror.

Dark eyes stared back at him from Rorgan Tyne's
face.

Disappointed, he flopped back onto the bed and
buried his face into his knees. 'No! No!' he cried,
feeling the threat of tears.

'We want to help you, Garry,' Pree Stappa said
urgently. 'This whole thing's just so amazing. Tell us
about yourself.'

Rubbing his eyes he studied the three children
sitting on the bed — Rorgan Tyne's bed. Pree Stappa,

27

freckled face, sandy hair, short, intelligent, obviously the leader; Drey Allenbow, the silent dark type, tall, moody perhaps, jealous of Rorgan Tyne; Marsimony Brin, younger than the rest, pretty, dark hair, fun.

Garry thought for a moment. Where to begin? There was so much to tell. He told them about his family, friends, school and Port Vlamingh. He described Aqua Mania and its new water slide. He told them that every day for two weeks before his birthday he'd received a pamphlet in the letterbox:

Why not slide down the Cannonball Chute on your next birthday? Ride the biggest, longest, most exciting water slide in the Southern Hemisphere.

'So I decided I would. I'd been to Aqua Mania plenty of times but this was a new slide that had just been built,' he concluded.

'And how did you meet Rorgan Tyne again?' asked Marsimony Brin, pushing back her long black hair.

Garry again related his meeting with the dark-haired boy on the Cannonball Chute. The children listened without interrupting, completely engrossed. Finally, Pree Stappa leaned back and said casually to the others, 'Well, we thought so, didn't we? At least that's one problem solved.'

'It is?' said Garry.

'Yes. You live in the same place we do,' replied Drey Allenbow.

Garry shook his head vigorously. 'No I don't. I've never seen you before or this diving complex with the Snake, or Trainer or Mother or ...'

'But it is only a *theory*, Pree Stappa. It's never been proved,' Marsimony Brin frowned.

'But it fits, doesn't it?' said Pree Stappa.

'Would someone please tell me what's going on?' cried Garry throwing his arms up in exasperation.

'Is our world sort of like your world, Garry?' asked Pree Stappa.

He glanced around the room. 'Well ... yes, I suppose so. I mean this is definitely a bedroom, only about a hundred times messier than mine. And you eat the same things and kind of dress the same and we speak the same language too. But you have people called "Trainer" and "Mother" and you've got strange names.'

Marsimony Brin giggled. 'Not as strange as yours! You've only got one name.'

He allowed a smile. 'No I haven't. Tenon is my surname — my family name — like Brin.'

She laughed again. 'My surname's Treloff but we hardly ever use surnames here. Brin's part of my first name.'

29

Garry nodded his understanding and turned to Pree Stappa. 'What you said before about our worlds being similar. Does that mean Port Vlamingh and Lennox City are the same place?'

'No, not the same *place*,' said Pree Stappa, her voice rising with excitement as she paced around the room, 'but they're in the same *space*. We share the same space.'

'But we can't!' cried Garry. 'How is it that I've never seen you before? How come that when I'm in Port Vlamingh I don't bump into you?'

'I know this sounds really incredible,' explained Drey Allenbow, 'but we live in the same space but in a different dimension.'

'You mean while I'm getting on with my day, you're doing the same, but I can't see you because we live in different dimensions? How can that be possible? I can't believe ... so it's sort of like going ...' Garry paused to find the right word.

'Sideways,' said Pree Stappa.

Garry shook his head in disbelief. 'This is fantastic ... but how do you know? Has this happened before?'

The three kids looked at each other.

'No,' said Pree Stappa. 'As far as we know you're the first. You see, last year, we had a fantastic teacher called Master who had some amazing ideas. He had a theory that there was a world in another dimension existing alongside ours. He thought its people were like us and spoke a similar language and reckoned he could get there by some sort of matter transference. He had a code name for it ... really strange ... something like ...' She hesitated trying to remember the name.

'Beady Eyes,' said Drey Allenbow.

'Beady eyes!' snorted Garry. 'Man oh man, now I've heard everything.'

'Yes, that's right, Beady Eyes.' Pree Stappa began prowling around the room again then turned to Marsimony Brin. 'Do you remember that?'

'Do I ever,' she replied. 'Kept going on about how he could use Beady Eyes to switch people's identities. Didn't stay long, did he? The Teachers Board sacked him.'

Garry held up his hands as though stopping traffic. 'Okay, okay, you've had your fun. You can drop the beady eyes thing. I don't believe a word of it.'

'We all thought he was crazy, of course, but Master was a great teacher. We all liked him,' said Pree Stappa, ignoring Garry's protests.

Drey Allenbow clicked his fingers. 'Including Rorgan Tyne,' he said slowly. 'He was the only teacher Rorgan Tyne got on with.'

'That's right,' said Marsimony Brin. 'Master also worked at the Pivot, remember? And Rorgan Tyne used to go up there and help him sometimes. Maybe they were working on the Beady Eyes theory.'

'HELLO!' cried Garry hopping out of bed and waving his arms in front of them. 'Is anybody listening? I said you can drop it now.'

Pree Stappa stopped pacing and stared at him. 'Do you want us to help, or not?'

'Yes, of course, but you're joking, aren't you? I mean, this beady eyes stuff. It sounds a bit ridiculous.'

'It might sound silly to you, Garry, but right now, it's your best hope,' she said coldly.

'Sorry.' Garry sat down on the bed again and scratched the skin on his knee. 'Look, I didn't mean to … okay, so supposing Rorgan Tyne and I switched places using this beady eyes thingy. What I don't understand is what's so significant about eyes that are beady?'

Drey Allenbow shrugged his shoulders. 'We wondered that, too. Maybe it's not important. Maybe we're reading too much into it.'

They fell silent, each contemplating the puzzle. Through the window, the sun shone brilliantly in a cloudless sky, promising a hot day. The only sound was the chirping of a cricket.

Suddenly Garry leaped up from the bed and raced to the mirror again, scrutinising Rorgan Tyne's reflection. Could it be possible? The hard, glassy black eyes stared back at him. He turned his head from side to side. Was it a trick of the light or did he see the eyes ... glitter? They were almost like — he stepped closer to the mirror — black beads!

'Look at my eyes!' Garry cried, swinging around to Marsimony Brin who had come up behind him to see what he was doing. 'Beady eyes!'

'You're right,' she said, studying his eyes. 'Funny, I've never noticed it before. They're shiny and cold just like a ...'

'Snake!' hissed Pree Stappa who had been staring out of the window towards the swimming pool.

They all looked at her, stunned.

'A snake,' she said again turning to face the kids, grinning broadly so the big freckles under her eyes stretched. 'Don't you see? A snake has beady eyes and,' she pointed towards the pool, 'we have a Snake in our own backyard.'

'Of course! The Snake!' breathed Drey Allenbow, clicking his fingers again. 'It makes sense, doesn't it?'

Garry looked doubtful. 'Does it?'

'Well it's beginning to,' said Pree Stappa. 'We know that the Master had a theory about switching places with someone in a different dimension and we also know he and Rorgan Tyne were pretty friendly. I bet the Master told Rorgan Tyne how to do it — how to switch places — and it involved sliding down the Snake.'

'But where do Rorgan Tyne's eyes come into this?' asked Garry.

'Did you look at his eyes when you met on the Cannonball Chute?' Drey Allenbow asked excitedly.

'Well, I guess I did. I remember thinking how black they were, that's all.'

'Energy transference,' said Drey Allenbow with an air of authority. 'He gave you some sort of power … with his eyes … his *beady eyes*.'

Garry shot him a withering look. 'Get real! That is ridiculous.'

'I'm not sure about Rorgan Tyne's eyes, Drey Allenbow,' said Pree Stappa, 'or if they've got anything to do with this. But I do think that beady eyes refers to the Snake and somehow that's the key to getting Garry home. Maybe there's a hidden tunnel or something.'

Drey Allenbow shrugged his shoulders.

Garry sighed. 'Look, what sort of guy is this Rorgan Tyne? Why would he want to switch places with me?'

'We don't know,' said Pree Stappa too quickly.

Garry looked at her but she wouldn't meet his eyes. What was she hiding?

'Well, can we ask the Master what to do?' he said.

Marsimony Brin shook her head vigorously so her ponytail swished from side to side. 'Like I said, he was sacked. We don't know where he is.'

'What about Trainer or Mother? They'd help, wouldn't they?'

'Whatever you do Garry, don't tell them,' warned Pree Stappa. 'They'd tell the authorities and then there'd be this huge investigation by the scientists. They'd want to study you and next thing, you'd be an exhibit in the museum. Then you'd never see Port Vlamingh again.'

Garry gulped. 'But won't they realise that I'm not Rorgan Tyne?'

'Don't worry about them. They're too busy thinking about the competition. If Rorgan Tyne's behaving himself, they'll be happy,' said Pree Stappa, smiling.

'What's the big deal about this competition?' asked Garry. 'And who's the guy … Lado Kaan … is that his name? The one who did the triple twist thingy?'

'Oh, he's a famous diver,' said Marsimony Brin. 'But he's a cripple now.'

'Poor guy. What happened to him?'

'A diving accident,' said Pree Stappa. 'You wanted to know about the competition?'

'Yes, and about Mother. Is she your real mother? Do you live here all the time? Do you go to school? Is Trainer your father?'

The kids burst out laughing. 'Not likely!' cried Marsimony Brin.

'First of all,' said Pree Stappa, pulling up the desk chair and sitting in front of Garry, 'normally we live with our families and go to schools in Lennox City. Twice a week after school we come here to train in an elite diving squad. Right now though, it's school holidays — two blissful weeks — and Trainer's running this live-in diving clinic so we can get some intensive tuition for the Diving Championships in a couple of months.'

Garry nodded. 'And ... Mother?'

'She's not our real mother. We just call her that because she's like a mum to us while we're here. Trainer's our ... well ... trainer ... and definitely *not* related!'

'So you don't mind giving up your holidays. I'd hate it. Yuck!' said Garry screwing up his nose.

Marsimony Brin laughed. 'No, we like it, really.'

'Well you've been down the Snake, Garry,' said Pree Stappa. 'It's fantastic, isn't it? And it's much better now we don't use mats.'

Drey Allenbow and Marsimony Brin nodded in agreement.

'What do you mean?' asked Garry.

'We used to go down on mats,' replied Drey Allenbow, 'before they redesigned the slide. Now jets of air push up tiny spurts of water through the slide. It's much easier to dive and a lot more exciting.'

'Yeah, ace fun,' said Garry, remembering the tickling fingers, 'like you're floating.'

Downstairs, the rattle of plates and cutlery signalled breakfast. Pree Stappa glanced at her watch. 'Time to go,' she announced. 'We always have something light to eat before we train. After that we'll work out how to get you home.'

'But what am I going to do?' asked Garry, panic rising in the pit of his stomach. 'I can't dive. Won't Trainer suspect something?'

Pree Stappa opened the bedroom door. 'Just do what you did yesterday. Follow us and don't say too much. Okay?' she whispered.

'Right,' said Garry, although he didn't feel very confident.

After they'd gone, he pondered the morning's events. What could *they* do? They were only kids. Sooner or later they'd have to tell an adult, wouldn't they? That's what *he* always did when he had a problem. Last year when Big Mikey gave him a black eye, didn't his mum sort it out? And when Andrew Simpson deliberately tripped him up at soccer he complained to the coach and Andrew was sent off. He just walked off the field and didn't come back — ever. Problem solved. Well, not quite. Andrew was the best player in the team and after he quit they didn't win a game all season. Maybe if *he'd* said something to Andrew ... maybe *he* could have sorted it out ... maybe ...

He shrugged his shoulders, put on his bathers which had dried overnight and pulled on some shorts and a shirt. He thought about the gigantic slide and a shiver of excitement ran down his spine as he made his way downstairs. Despite his predicament he was really looking forward to riding the Snake again. And maybe this time he'd slip through some hidden tunnel like Pree Stappa said and slide back to Aqua Mania.

He just *had* to have a quick look at the Snake before breakfast.

Garry stopped at the front door as Mother and the kids appeared from the kitchen. She was explaining something, her voice high, tense, urgent. She looked up as he turned the door handle.

'Don't go outside, Rorgan Tyne!' he heard her gasp. 'It might be dangerous!'

But it was too late. Garry stepped outside into the brilliant sunshine and stood admiring the Snake.

It was a clear morning, and hot. The Snake curled majestically over the enticing water of the swimming pool. There was nothing to be frightened of. Why had Mother told him not to go outside? Boy it was hot!

Garry smiled. He had a plan. Today he'd ride the Snake again and again and again until he slipped through that secret exit back into Aqua Mania. Then he'd find Rorgan Tyne and swap places ... somehow. But first — breakfast. He was starving!

Turning, he was amazed to see Mother and the kids at the kitchen window, yelling at him through the glass and beckoning.

Mother met him at the door and pulled him inside. 'Rorgan Tyne, are you all right?' she asked anxiously as they made their way into the kitchen. The kids sat at the table helping themselves to toast.

'Of course I am. Why?' Garry looked warily at Pree Stappa.

'Is it hot outside? It looks hot,' said Mother.

'Yes. Why?'

'Hotter than yesterday?'

'Yes.' What was she on about?

'It's happening quicker than they thought it would.'

'What is? What are you talking about?'

'The Modulator has malfunctioned,' said Mother. 'They're working on it but the temperature could reach dangerous levels. You must all stay inside until the danger's over. I'll call Trainer … see if I can find out some more details.' And she bustled off.

Garry turned to the kids. 'What modulator? What's she talking about?'

'The Modulator is the computer that controls our weather,' explained Pree Stappa urgently. 'It's never failed before. This is very serious.'

'You're joking!' cried Garry. 'Are you telling me that …?'

'Shh! Keep your voice down!' hissed Pree Stappa, waving her toast at him. 'Mother will hear.'

'A *computer* controls the weather?' he whispered.

'Of course. If it didn't we wouldn't survive under the shell.'

'What shell? What are you talking about?'

'Up there,' said Pree Stappa pointing out of the window to the sky, 'is a huge domed shell that covers Lennox City.'

Garry peered up into the perfect blue sky. 'Where? I can't see it.'

'It's there, really. Every day hundreds of storms bombard Lennox City. If you look really closely, you can sometimes see streaks of lightning hitting the shell and ricocheting off ... there ... did you see that?'

'Yes!' cried Garry. 'And there's another one!'

'What you're seeing is the weather outside the shell. Sometimes the temperature's minus forty degrees. Then in an instant, it's boiling hot or it suddenly pelts down with hail or there's a violent storm. If we didn't have the shell we'd cop it all. There'd be no way we'd survive.'

'But has the shell always been there?'

'No. Our ancestors settled here way before the storms came. But then over the next two hundred years the weather patterns worsened. About fifty years ago they constructed the shell and the first Modulator, and they've rebuilt them as the technology's developed.'

'Are there other cities like this with shells?'

'No, only ours.' She swept her hand towards the unseen horizon. 'Beyond our shell the land is no longer habitable because of the storms.'

'Wow! So where is the computer — the Modulator? What does it do?'

'It's in the Pivot — the control tower in the middle of the city. Although the shell protects us it also blocks out the climate changes we need. That's why we have the Modulator. It's programmed to harness parts of the outside weather, convert them to data and store them in its memory. Every day the Modulator converts data into weather. For example, when we need water for our crops to grow, the computer converts the "rain" data back into rain. When we need dry weather for harvesting, that's what the computer gives us.'

'Does it ever snow?' asked Garry.

'I think the Modulator collects snow data but it's never been used.'

'Until today,' he said, pointing towards the window. 'Look at that!'

'What is *that*?' gasped Marsimony Brin.

He grinned. 'Snow! Come on!'

Garry ran to the door, the other three following. A blast of cold air rushed in as he opened the door. Already the ground was completely covered in snow. He sprang into the whiteness, picked up handfuls of it and threw snowballs at the kids. Soon all four of them were throwing snowballs, laughing and getting thoroughly wet.

But as quickly as the snow had appeared, it disappeared. Sudden heat pounded down ferociously and within minutes steaming pools of water were all that was left of the snow. Quickly they scampered inside to escape the heat.

Marsimony Brin flicked the last of the melted snow from her ponytail. 'That was fantastic!'

'You should have seen your face when I belted you with that snowball, Pree Stappa,' laughed Garry, and he pulled a face to show the others. Drey Allenbow collapsed onto the floor with laughter and Marsimony Brin went into a fit of giggles.

'Children!' Mother stood in the doorway. She seemed completely oblivious to the children's laughter and damp clothing. 'I've just heard on the news. They know why the Modulator failed.'

The kids stood silent, their fun forgotten and the seriousness of the situation remembered.

'What's happened?' asked Pree Stappa.

'One of the components is missing,' she said. 'It's called the Link. It's quite small — about the size of a watch face but thicker — and has magnetic properties that channel the outside weather to the databanks. Without it the Modulator's going crazy, converting data it doesn't need to.'

'What do they think's happened to it?'

'It was stolen.'

'Stolen! Who'd want to do something like that? It's a bit sick isn't it?' Pree Stappa screwed up her freckled nose in disgust. 'Do they know who did it?'

'No idea.'

'Why don't they just put in another Link?' asked Drey Allenbow.

'There isn't one. The Link is an ancient rock brought by a meteor shower before the shell was built. It's the only one that was ever found.'

'But didn't they try to duplicate it in case its properties weakened or it got damaged or … stolen?'

Mother shrugged her muscular shoulders. 'Apparently they tried but never got it right. After a while they realised it wasn't losing its power and as for being stolen — the whole of the Pivot is under tight security.'

'Not tight enough, apparently,' said Pree Stappa. 'So what's going to happen to us?'

Mother sighed. 'Well, until the police find the stolen Link, I'm afraid we must move to the subcaves.'

'It's that serious?' asked Marsimony Brin.

A noise like a million feet tap dancing on a tin roof silenced her. They raced to the window. Hailstones as big as tennis balls bounced onto the ground. Then just as suddenly the phenomenal noise stopped and there was a weird stillness.

Within seconds, as they watched, the hail melted and an intense heat drove them away from the window. In shocked silence they each contemplated the catastrophe that lay ahead if the Link was not found. Without the usual weather patterns, crops and livestock would die. Storms would soon destroy the houses. Electricity, water, gas and sewage connections would not last long and diseases would rise and spread. Provisions in the subcaves would eventually run out. Beyond Lennox City lay a wasteland crippled by the constant bombardment of storms, so evacuation to this hostile land was out of the question. The children stared at each other, white-faced and wide-eyed in disbelief. If the Link wasn't found they would all die.

Garry looked out the window, shading his eyes from the heat. You could fry an egg on those bricks and probably boil an egg in the swimming pool water. And in an instant the temperature would drop and the egg would freeze. Now more than ever he wanted to get back to Port Vlamingh. No matter what the weather was like he had to get into the Snake and find a way out. But there was something else nagging at him. It was something Mother had said.

Something about the Link ... a watch face ... something to do with Rorgan Tyne ... what was it?

Back upstairs the question gnawed at Garry as he sat on his bed watching the ever-changing seasons out of the window. It was good to have some time to think. During the morning, he and the others had helped Mother pack provisions to take to the subcave. By late morning, Drey Allenbow and Marsimony Brin had been picked up by their parents.

In the street below, car horns blared and tense voices shouted. Garry watched a procession of vehicles, people and animals making their way through the streets, presumably to the subcaves. Where were these shelters and how large were they? Could they hold the whole population of Lennox City?

Pree Stappa was in her room packing. That's what *he* was supposed to be doing, too, of course, but what was the point? He wasn't going anywhere with a suitcase full of Rorgan Tyne's stuff. The only travelling he intended to do was through the secret passage in the Snake and back to Port Vlamingh.

He'd panicked when Mother had said their parents were on their way to collect them. Fortunately, Rorgan Tyne's dad wasn't coming until the afternoon and hopefully the build-up of traffic would delay him further.

Garry suddenly jumped up from the bed. What was he doing staring at the weather? He had to get out there and find a way through the Snake before Rorgan Tyne's dad came for him. What would he need? Quickly! He looked around the untidy room. A jacket in case it rained or snowed — yes. A pair of sneakers and jeans. He put these on. What else? A pen — no; a water pistol — definitely not; a pocketknife on a gold chain — could come in handy. He threw it around his neck. A broken leather watch covering — no … wait …

Garry paused, willing himself to remember. There was something important. Here was that feeling again … something to do with the missing Link and Rorgan Tyne … and this waterproof watchstrap. He closed his eyes and thought about his meeting with Rorgan Tyne so long ago. No! It was only yesterday! And then he remembered the black leather band on Rorgan Tyne's wrist. Could it be?

He raced from the bedroom and hammered on

Pree Stappa's door until she opened it. He held up the leather strap. 'Pree Stappa. Look!'

'Garry, I'm really sorry all this has happened,' she said, absent-mindedly taking the strap and ushering him into her room.

'But ...'

'I said I'd help you to get back to Port Vlamingh but ... my mother will be here to collect me soon. You're on your own now ... I'm sorry ... why did you give me this?' She held up the waterproof watchstrap.

'The Link!' Garry exclaimed. 'I think Rorgan Tyne stole it!'

Pree Stappa's eyes widened, her freckles stood out on her pale face. 'How do you know? What's this old strap got to do with it?'

'Rorgan Tyne was wearing something like it on the water slide.'

'So? He wears his new one because this one's had the bomb. So what?'

'But don't you see? Mother said the Link was about the size of a watch face only thicker. Could Rorgan Tyne have stolen it from the ... Pivot thingy ... and hidden it on his wrist under the waterproof strap?'

'It's possible, I suppose. He might have known about the Link and where to find it. Master could have shown him.'

Garry shrugged his shoulders. 'It's too much of a coincidence, isn't it? Him and the Link disappearing at the same time?'

'Maybe,' said Pree Stappa as she paced the room.

'You think he did it?'

'I said, maybe.'

'But,' continued Garry, 'why would he do something like this? I mean, why would he put everyone in danger?'

'Perhaps he didn't realise the danger.'

'So you *do* think it was him!'

Pree Stappa sat on the bed. Around her lay clothes and books, a suitcase half filled. She fidgeted with the leather strap, silent. Garry felt sure she wasn't telling him something.

'Okay, spit it out, Pree Stappa,' he said. 'What are you hiding from me?'

'Well,' she said, screwing up her face, 'well … Rorgan Tyne is a bit … different … eccentric maybe. But he can really dive. He is *so* gifted. And he's clever at other things too. He likes manipulating language. Playing with words. You know what I mean?'

Garry nodded.

'But,' she continued, 'we don't get on with him. He does stupid things and lets the team down. You already know that.' She continued piling things into the suitcase.

'Yes, go on.'

'Well, this morning you asked me why Rorgan Tyne would want to switch places and I said I didn't know. Well I think I'm partly to blame. You see, a couple of weeks ago I was so annoyed with him that I told him he shouldn't be on the team. He said one day he'd leave and I'd be sorry. I think he really hated us all and just wanted to disappear and never come back.'

She looked up at Garry. 'I'm *really* sorry. I thought when he said he'd leave, he'd go *home*, not vanish into your world. I certainly didn't think he'd steal something like the Link or drag you into this. He said I'd be sorry and I am!' She angrily threw the last of her clothes into the suitcase.

'It's not your fault, Pree Stappa. He sounds like he's a bit cracked or something,' said Garry, picking up some books that had fallen on the floor.

'What will you do now, Garry?'

'I'm going to get out of here, find Rorgan Tyne and get back into my body.'

'And if Rorgan Tyne has the Link?' she asked quietly.

There was an awkward silence. He looked at her, hot with shame that he had momentarily forgotten the plight of Lennox City and thought only of himself. If he were right about the Link then only he could save these people from — he didn't even want to think the word — death. The magnitude of responsibility crawled slowly through his stomach like hot lava and he felt sick.

'If he did steal it I'll try to make sure he returns it, but I can't promise,' he said lamely.

'I know, I just thought … never mind … look Garry, they've switched off the electricity so there won't be any water in the Snake. 'You'll need to use …'

BANG! The house shook violently as Pree Stappa and Garry rushed to the window. Gentle snow drifted down onto the white-carpeted streets. Two cars, their drivers unfamiliar with the icy conditions, had crashed. A dog in the back of one car yelped frantically.

Garry didn't hesitate. He dashed down the stairs and into the street to help.

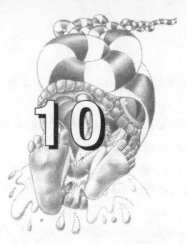

Sudden heat blasted Garry and puddles of water slowly turned into steaming mini saunas. Heart racing madly, he darted across the road to the crashed cars, narrowly avoiding a splash of hot water spewed up by the wheels of a passing car.

A crowd had gathered and he pushed his way to the front, eager to get a better view of the dog. Two men were trying to lever open a car door to free the drivers. The man was unconscious ... or dead. The other driver, blood trickling down his forehead, was being helped from his seat and into a wheelchair which someone had pulled from the front of the vehicle. The kelpie paced the back seat of the car, whining. It was tethered by its lead.

'For goodness sake!' the driver yelled at a woman who was trying to help him. 'I'm all right. Stop fussing.'

'I'm taking you into my house,' said the woman, turning the chair around and pushing the angry man towards the footpath. 'There's a cut on your head. It'll need attention.'

'I don't want your help!' protested the man. 'Take your hands off my chair! Someone get that mongrel of a dog out! Turn me around at once! Turn me around ...' His voice trailed off as he disappeared into the house.

The kelpie continued to howl. The air suddenly became stifling and the crowd dispersed quickly, unable to bear the heat. Garry couldn't stand it. If nobody else would help this poor dog, he would. Frantically he scrambled through the driver's door, leaned over to the back seat and pulled at the lead tied to the door handle. It wouldn't come loose. Grabbing the kelpie's collar, he unclipped the lead and the dog bounded past him through the door and over to the shade of a tree.

Garry followed, wiping the sweat from his forehead with his sleeve. 'Good fella,' he murmured as he stroked the dog behind the ears. But it cowered and backed away, trembling. 'You're okay, just a bit of a fright, I think.' The dog growled, put its head on one side and looked up at Garry with bewildered eyes. Then it sniffed at his hand and sat whimpering at his feet.

Garry squatted next to it and patted its head. 'I have to go, fella. Better go back to your owner, now.

Off you go.' But the dog followed him as he hurried past the crashed cars, back to the swimming complex.

He stopped at the front door and the kelpie lay down, head on its front paws. Garry surveyed the chaos in the street. What was he doing? Was he mad? Saving a dog's life when he had his own to worry about! Why was he wasting precious time? He glanced at his watch. It was midday. He had to get out of here. Rorgan Tyne's dad could arrive any time now. Then he remembered … Pree Stappa … she'd been telling him something about the Snake.

Pree Stappa wasn't in her room upstairs and neither was her suitcase. She wasn't anywhere. While he'd been rescuing the dog, her mum must have collected her he decided. She hadn't even said goodbye. Odd. But this whole place was odd and he had to get out … NOW!

He heard loud voices coming from downstairs. He couldn't go that way. What if it was Rorgan Tyne's dad? He darted back to the bedroom and flung open the window. A hot wind seared his face and flung back his stringy black hair.

It was a long way down but that was the only way out now.

'Rorgan Tyne!' called Mother from downstairs.

This was it. He had to go now. Hurry! He had to get out of here!

Gingerly, he put one leg over the windowsill, then the other and sat in the heat looking for a way down. It was too far to jump. He turned around to face the open window and lowered himself down, his dancing feet finally resting on a narrow ledge. He reached to his left and grabbed a downpipe, wrapped his legs around it and quickly slid down the metal. It was scorching!

On the ground he ran until he reached the lift at the base of the Snake. There he crouched, panting, blowing on his burnt hands. The temperature dropped suddenly and over the hard, continuous drumming of the rain, he thought he heard Mother calling to him. He pressed the button on the lift. Nothing happened.

'It isn't working, Garry,' said a voice behind him.

He whirled around. 'Pree Stappa! I thought you'd gone.'

'I thought *you'd* gone! While you were attending to the sick and wounded,' she jibed, 'I took my bags down to the kitchen and waited for you. When you didn't come back I thought you'd gone straight to the Snake. So I came looking for you. How's the dog?'

'Frightened but okay. It kept following me. What about the Snake? You were telling me something about it.' Suddenly the rain turned to hail, then snow.

'Come here!' she said pulling him through a doorway into a dark room. It took several seconds for Garry's eyes to adjust to the dim light. Beyond it was another small room and in front of him, a set of stairs. He guessed they led up to the Snake. There was an eerie silence.

Pree Stappa reached into a box at the foot of the stairs and pulled out a pair of soft rubber boots, the soles covered in small suction pads.

'You'll need these. We use them when we're cleaning the inside of the Snake. It gets pretty slippery in there, even without water, and the suction pads help to get a grip. You can walk upside down too,' she grinned.

Garry took the boots and smiled even though his teeth were chattering with the cold.

Pree Stappa sprinted up the stairs. 'Come on!' she yelled.

Clutching the boots, Garry followed her. They raced up the stairs, jostling each other in a bid to be first. Puffing, they reached the top together and stood looking at the world below them with amazement.

'Wow!' exclaimed Garry, clouds of vapour tumbling from his mouth. His eyes followed the Snake's slithering form down to the ice-encrusted pool and beyond. Lennox City was shrouded in snow. It was beautiful. Like the Christmas cards his grandparents sent from England.

'But look at all the people leaving their homes,' said Pree Stappa sadly as she pointed to the red tail-lights of cars weaving towards the city's underground shelters.

'Oh-oh,' said Garry in alarm. 'Quick, Pree Stappa! Down!'

They both crouched near the Snake's entrance. The back door of the house had opened and someone was coming out.

'Rorgan Tyne!' called a voice. The name echoed around the empty courtyard.

They peeped over the top of the Snake. The man in the wheelchair had a bandage around his head and a kelpie sniffed the snow at his feet.

Garry was astonished. 'But that's ...'

'Rorgan Tyne's father,' said Pree Stappa pulling Garry down out of sight.

'Rorgan Tyne! Stop fooling around and come here now!' the man bellowed.

'But,' whispered Garry, 'he was in the crash. I rescued his dog.'

'That was *him*? Did he see you?'

'No, I don't think so ... what happened to him ... why is he ...?'

'In a wheelchair? Diving accident ... long time ago.'

There was silence. Garry's brain raced. He peeked again at the man who was trying unsuccessfully to move the wheelchair through the snow.

'That's Lado Kaan, isn't it?' he said slowly.

'Yes.'

'And he's Rorgan Tyne's father?'

'Yes.'

'Blast this snow!' shouted Lado Kaan. 'Rorgan Tyne, help me!'

Lado Kaan was stuck. The snow had iced up around the wheels of the chair and there was no traction at all. 'Rorgan Tyne!' he called angrily, thrashing his arms about. His hand struck the kelpie's nose and it scampered out of the way, whimpering.

Garry flinched involuntarily. 'Poor dog.'

'Look, I'll go and help Lado Kaan,' whispered Pree Stappa. 'I'll take him inside and that will give you time to go down the Snake.'

'What will you tell him about me ... I mean, about Rorgan Tyne?'

'I'll think of something. Now get going.' She turned to go.

'Pree Stappa, wait!'

'What is it?'

'I said I'd try to send Rorgan Tyne back with the Link but if I can't I'll return it myself — that's if he's got it.' He gulped at the enormity of this statement.

She beamed. 'Thanks, Garry. I was hoping you would. I'll tell the authorities everything. They'll be waiting here at the Snake.'

'No, don't. We could still be wrong about all of this.'

'I don't think we are. We have to tell the police.'

'No. Let's be sure first before we say anything. I don't want to involve them and then discover we've made a mistake.'

Pree Stappa shrugged. 'If that's what you want.' She drew a silver necklace over her head and pushed it into his hand. 'Here, wear this.'

'What for?'

'So I don't get confused. If you come back, I'll know it's you, no matter who you look like. Now go!' She waved to him and disappeared down the steps.

Garry secured the chain around his neck and watched the dog sniff the ground before wandering off. Hastily he pulled on the rubber boots and waited until Pree Stappa had wheeled the man back inside. His thoughts raced. Had Rorgan Tyne taken the Link? Why? He must be a really mixed-up kid to have done that! Why had he chosen him, Garry, to change places with? Was it chance or had he been chosen deliberately? Concentrate ... concentrate ... find a way out. Get back into the right body and send Rorgan Tyne back here to save Lennox City. But how?

He stepped into the entrance of the waterless

Snake. The boots gripped the surface and made loud slurping noises each time he moved. Slowly, he inched along the tunnel using his hands to push at the curved wall. Rain was pelting down again and then hail. Huge chunks of ice hammered the Snake and the noise was deafening. What was he looking for? Would he know it when he found it? He searched every loop, every corner. He walked upside down like a fly. He pushed, prodded, probed and pounded the walls. Nothing. The tunnel was seamless. And eventually he came to the exit and peered down to the cold water of the pool.

He lay there, on his stomach, bitterly disappointed. There was something missing. Something he'd overlooked, but he couldn't think what it was. He pictured himself flying down the Cannonball Chute and then being catapulted into the water. Something had happened just before the exit. What was it? What *was* it?

A tingling sensation. No … tickling … after the mat had slipped from under him he'd felt the water tickling his body. He looked closely at the floor of the Snake. Thousands of tiny holes patterned the surface. That's where the jets of water were coming from … the tickling of the water! He'd felt it because … he didn't have … a mat!

Was that it? The *mat*? Should he be looking for a

mat instead of a secret passage? He remembered the moment in the queue for the Cannonball Chute when he'd been pushed and had lost his mat. Rorgan Tyne had handed it back. *You'll go faster*, he'd said. Or had he swapped mats? Garry wasn't sure. But surely all this must have something to do with the mat Rorgan Tyne had given him. If he used it again maybe he'd get back home. After all, Rorgan Tyne must have used it to escape this place. Garry scrambled up the inside of the gigantic slide, the rubber boots slurping rudely.

Emerging from the tunnel, he peeled off the boots and ran down the stairs to the little room at the bottom. Was it a storeroom? Trainer's command from yesterday rang in his ears: *Pree Stappa, put that mat in the storeroom!* Garry's heart sang with jubilation. He was going home! He knew it. He flung open the storeroom door and squinted into the small dark room. But his euphoria turned to dismay. Along one wall, stacked to the ceiling, were what seemed like hundreds of mats.

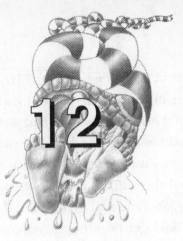

12

Garry couldn't believe it. Just when he was sure he was going home, there it was. Defeat. How could he possibly know which mat was Rorgan Tyne's? It would take months to try out all these. Angrily he kicked at the pile and a thick cloud of dust puffed up in his face. Hang on. These mats hadn't been used for ages. Hadn't Pree Stappa said they didn't use them anymore? He peered at the top row of mats which had been tossed carelessly in place. Someone had thrown them up there from the ground. Had Pree Stappa thrown Rorgan Tyne's mat up there too?

He dragged a rickety table across the room and climbed on it. He could just reach the top of the mats. He ran his finger along each mat, inspecting his hand for dust. Each mat was filthy except the last one.

'Gotcha!' he whispered, grasping the handles and pulling it towards him. Not a speck of dust. It was still even a bit wet. This was the one.

Hurriedly he climbed off the teetering table and raced out of the storeroom. Back at the entrance of the Snake a savage wind almost knocked him to the ground and he grasped the sides of the tunnel to stop himself being blown over the safety rail. The Snake shook violently in the wind. Garry thought he could hear it hissing with displeasure.

Was it safe? Could he slide down the Snake when there was no water running through it? Did it matter? His choices were pretty limited. He could stay here and definitely die or he could go down the Snake and maybe die. Exhausted, he closed his eyes and stretched himself out on the mat at the entrance.

But he had the feeling he was not alone and turned sharply to see the dog sitting at his side.

'Following me again are you fella?' he said gently. 'Can't take you with me.'

He didn't remember pushing off with his hands but perhaps the wind forced him forwards. Next thing, he was sliding fast on the mat. Faster and faster. He felt dizzy. Down, down, down. Around loops, swirling around corners. Faster, faster. Then no more light, just darkness and the familiar smell of chlorine as water splashed over his face.

A tremendous roar filled his ears and then WHOOOOOSH! A brilliant flash of coloured light exploded in front of him. He was no longer sliding but floating gently on his back, water licking his arms and legs. Happy voices echoed around him. Delicious smells of Aqua Mania food wafted up his nostrils. He didn't dare open his eyes. What if his mind was playing tricks? What if he was still in Lennox City?

'Hurry up, get out of there!'

He opened his eyes. Light blinded him and he held up a hand to shield his face from the early afternoon sun. A pool attendant was motioning to him to get out of the water. This was no trick. This was Aqua Mania.

'Yes!' he yelled with relief, punching the air and dragging himself out of the shallow pool, narrowly avoiding another kid who had just come down the Cannonball Chute.

'Watch out, weirdo,' said the kid, flicking Garry's jacket.

Garry looked down and realised he was still wearing Rorgan Tyne's jeans, jacket and shoes. He must look ridiculous! No wonder people were staring. Any other time he would have died with embarrassment. Today, he was happy to be here. Happy to be alive.

Clutching the precious mat to his side, he stepped over the pool wall and ran his hand over his wet face. He fingered the scar on his chin and explored his smooth even teeth with his tongue. He may be alive but he was still in Rorgan Tyne's skin, of course. They would both have to ride the slide together to switch identities.

The delicious aroma of meat pies wafted from the kiosk. Garry's stomach rumbled and his mouth watered. Boy, he was starving! He wanted to find Rorgan Tyne but he was so weak with hunger he knew he couldn't do another thing until he'd eaten. But he had no money, so he hung around the tables and watched a large woman and an equally obese child tucking into a big bucket of chips and coke. Eventually the pair stood up and waddled off, leaving a pile of soggy chips.

Garry didn't waste any time. He squelched over to the table in his soaking joggers, flung his jacket over a chair to dry, shooed away a couple of scavenging seagulls and hungrily devoured the remains. Finally he sat back and gave a contented burp. It was a loud burp, more explosive than he'd anticipated, and the lady at the next table turned round and shot him a disapproving look. But he was so happy to be back in his own world he didn't care what people thought of him. His clothes were beginning to dry, he had the mat and now all he had to do was walk home — it would take an hour or so at least, he reckoned — find Rorgan Tyne, swap places and send him back to Lennox City with the Link. Easy-peasy after everything he'd been through.

Garry picked up the jacket and mat and made his way towards the exit.

'Ah, young man,' said a woman at the gate, 'you'll need to leave *that* here.'

Garry stared at her. What was she talking about?

'The mat, dear, it belongs to us,' she smiled pleasantly.

'Oh, the mat,' Garry said thinking fast. 'Actually, it's mine. I brought it with me.'

'No, dear, I think you'll find it belongs to us,' said the woman testily as she tried to grab the mat.

Garry hugged it tightly to his chest. *She* might think it was Aqua Mania's but *he* knew it wasn't. They struggled for several seconds then Garry did something he would never have done under normal circumstances. He kicked her.

'OUCH!' yelled the woman, letting go of the mat. She fell backwards to the floor and sat clutching her ankle. 'Security! *Security!*' she screamed.

Garry dodged around some amused onlookers and ran.

When he was a safe distance from Aqua Mania, he stopped to catch his breath and plan his next move. First, find Rorgan Tyne … find out how and why he'd switched places with him … so far, so good. Tell him about the effect of the Modulator not working. Convince him that he can save Lennox City by returning with the stolen Link. Oh sure! He wouldn't buy that. Why should he? Why would Rorgan Tyne go back and risk being punished for stealing? And causing destruction of catastrophic proportions?

Garry shook his head and began walking again. This was not going to be as easy as he'd originally thought. What if Rorgan Tyne just laughed at him and said he was never going back? What would happen to him then? He'd be stuck in this Rorgan Tyne skin forever! He'd have no home, nothing to prove that he was Garry Tenon. Legally he didn't even exist! And what had Rorgan Tyne been doing to his life in the last twenty-four hours? He didn't even want to think about that. Sweat trickled down his forehead as he trudged along the coastal road.

It took him much longer than he'd anticipated and by the time he reached home the afternoon Spring light was fading. A boy was cycling down the road towards him and as he came nearer, Garry recognised his friend Cameron who lived next door. Cameron would help him! Why hadn't he thought of that before?

'Hi!' Garry called, waving.

A blare from a car horn drowned out his greeting. Cameron didn't even seem to see him as he swung his bike into his yard where a car was backing out of the drive. He leaned the bike up against the side of the house and jumped into the waiting car which sped off, tail-lights twinkling red in the dusk.

Garry stood in the middle of the road watching the disappearing car. Well, it wouldn't have worked anyway. What would he have said? *Hi Cameron. How ya doing? Guess what? I'm really your friend, Garry. I know I don't look like him but it's a long story.* Oh yeah. Sure. Better stick to plan A: Find Rorgan Tyne.

Headlights from a car suddenly swept up the street and Garry scrambled out of sight behind a bush in his front garden. It was a police car and it was pulling into his drive. Garry crouched lower, waiting, listening.

A tall thin police officer got out and adjusted her hat.

'Come on, young man,' she said leaning over to speak to the passenger. 'Let's talk to your parents.'

Peering through the bushes, Garry watched a boy climb reluctantly from the car and amble towards the front door. A shiver of alarm ran down Garry's spine. That mop of curly blond hair was unmistakable. The boy was him, or rather, it was Rorgan Tyne in *his* body! It was the weirdest thing, watching himself yet knowing that it wasn't him.

Garry's mum opened the door and a shaft of light spilled out onto the silhouetted figures. Snatches of conversation drifted into the night and Garry held his breath, listening.

'Mrs Tenon? I'm Senior Constable Judy Parvin.'

'Yes … what's happened?'

Garry's mum leaned over and ruffled Rorgan Tyne's mop of blond hair. Garry smiled to himself as Rorgan Tyne ducked out of the way. That's exactly what he did, too. His mother was always doing that to him. It was incredibly annoying.

'Get off!' Rorgan Tyne complained, slapping her hand away and storming inside.

'Please come in,' Garry heard his mother say. 'He's not usually like this. My husband and I are very worried …' Then her voice trailed off as she ushered the constable inside and closed the door.

Garry felt wretched. It was like a huge hand had grabbed his guts and twisted the life out of him. He couldn't bear to hear the pain in his mother's voice, the despair, the disappointment. What on earth had Rorgan Tyne done?

He crept up to the window of the lounge room. He could hear only muffled sounds, voices rising and falling. Presently the front door opened once more and the police officer came out.

'Thank you, Mr Tenon. We'll be in touch,' she said, getting into the police car and driving off.

Garry wanted to run to the door and scream, *Dad, Dad it's me!* But how ridiculous would that be? How would he explain everything that had happened? He couldn't even explain it to himself, let alone his dad.

He waited in the shadows by the house. A full moon rose and cast a silvery light across the lawn. He had to get to Rorgan Tyne tonight and convince him to switch places. Turning to creep around the back of the house to his room, he was startled by a figure hurrying towards him. It looked like him but of course it was Rorgan Tyne.

He carried Garry's backpack and seemed to be running away.

Garry leaned the mat up against the side of the house, well hidden behind a bush. As Rorgan Tyne hurried past, Garry leaped out from the shadows and sprang onto him. THUD! The boy sprawled to the ground with Garry on top of him.

'What the ...!'

'Shh!' Garry hissed, sitting on Rorgan Tyne's back and pinning his arms to the ground. 'You've got a lot of explaining to do!'

'It's you!' Rorgan Tyne whispered, recognising his own voice.

'Right first time.'

'How did you get here?'

'Never mind that! You and I have to talk.'

Garry stood up and pulled Rorgan Tyne up by the arm, twisting it hard against the pack on his back. Together they stumbled across the moonlit backyard towards the garden shed. It was used to store old furniture and was never locked.

'Okay. Explain,' said Garry once they were inside. He watched, fascinated, as Rorgan Tyne shrugged his shoulders and rubbed the arm that Garry had pushed behind his back. It was so weird. This kid was a carbon copy of him except that his mouth sagged at the corners in a permanent frown. Maybe he wasn't used to the braces on his teeth. Garry's eyes rested on the watchstrap that he thought concealed the Link.

'How did you get here?' asked Rorgan Tyne, shaking his head in disbelief. 'How did you work out ...?'

'Why did you switch places with me?' interrupted Garry. 'Why did you trick me?'

'Oh, poor, poor little Garry,' sneered Rorgan Tyne, regaining his composure. He pulled off the backpack and settled himself into a rocking chair.

Garry sat down next to him on a stool. 'You'd better not sit on that chair. It's broken.'

'I don't care.'

'Suit yourself. Now, why switch places with me?'

Rorgan Tyne ran his hand through his curly mass of hair and sniffed. 'Had to get away, that's all.' He shifted uncomfortably on the rocking chair.

'Why?'

'My intellectual talents were wasted in Lennox City. Wanted to start a new life. Everybody picked on me, especially those kids. I didn't like them, they didn't like me. The only one that cared about me was that stupid dog of mine.'

'The kelpie?'

'Yeah. Mongrel of an animal, isn't it? Needs a firm hand. You have to show them who's boss, you know.'

Garry knew now why the dog had followed him, despite the mistreatment it obviously endured from Rorgan Tyne. It thought Garry was its owner. No wonder it had looked so bewildered when he'd patted and comforted it. Rorgan Tyne would never have done that.

'So anyway,' continued Rorgan Tyne, 'those losers were always getting me into trouble. It wasn't *my* fault.' He paused and looked up, daring Garry to contradict him.

'But you're a brilliant diver.'

'Of course I am, but I hate it.'

'Nobody's *making* you dive, though.'

Rorgan Tyne snorted. 'You obviously haven't met my father.'

'So the talented Rorgan Tyne ran away?' Garry said sarcastically.

'Ran away! That's kids' stuff. If you must know, I planned my escape months in advance, right down to the last detail.'

In spite of his anger, Garry was intrigued. 'And somehow that plan included me?'

'You're catching on, kiddo,' Rorgan Tyne said. He rocked gently back and forth like a contented old man. The chair creaked.

'Why? Why *me*?'

'Ah!' said Rorgan Tyne, eyes reflecting the moonlight so he looked slightly crazy. He stopped rocking and leaned forward. 'Haven't worked that one out yet, huh? Notice anything about our names?'

'Garry ... Rorgan Tyne,' mused Garry. 'Not really.'

'What about the *letters* in each name?'

The letters? What was he on about? Garry frowned.

Rorgan Tyne rolled his eyes and sighed theatrically. 'Rorgan Tyne ... Garry Tenon. If you rearrange the letters ...'

'Man oh man! An anagram!'

'Yes, I decided to swap places with someone whose name contained the same letters as mine.'

'Why?'

'Why not? I thought it'd be fun.'

Garry raised his eyebrows. 'But you didn't have to?'

'No, but I wanted the challenge. And I found you. Sheer genius.'

'Sheer luck more like it. The chances of you

meeting me at Aqua Mania must be one in a million!'

'Give me credit, Garry. It wasn't *chance*. Like I said, I planned it.'

'What?'

'I've been to Port Vlamingh loads of times. The hard part was finding you, then it was easy,' boasted Rorgan Tyne.

'So how *did* you find me?'

Rorgan Tyne sat up in the rocking chair and rubbed his hands together. He was obviously enjoying this. 'Well, first I rearranged the letters of my name to find all the variations. Let me see, there was Ryan Torgen, Ryan Gerton, Tory Ganner, Arron Genty, Regan Norty … I liked that one!' He paused and grinned, the braces on his teeth glinting in the moonlight. 'Roy Gannert, Tony Ranger and, of course, Garry Tenon.'

'But there'd be hundreds of names!'

'Yes, then I came here and searched telephone directories and electoral rolls and anything else I could get hold of to find people with the right surnames. Then I snooped around asking questions about their kids.'

'And you found me.'

'After a lot of searching, yes. It was easy finding people with a matching surname. But finding a kid with the right first name — that was a challenge. I really wanted to find a Regan Norty, of course. He sounded like fun.'

'But how did you know I'd be at Aqua Mania? It's not like I hang out there every week.'

'Garry, Garry, Garry,' said Rorgan Tyne, shaking his head. 'I'm *so* disappointed in you. I thought you'd be able to work *that* one out. It's so simple and yet so ingenious.'

'What are you talking about?'

Rorgan Tyne rocked in the chair, arms folded. 'Did you think it was just *coincidence* that you got all those pamphlets in the mail just before your birthday?'

There was silence. Garry recalled the weeks leading up to his birthday.

'We got a leaflet from Aqua Mania every day for two weeks.' He remembered the opening sentence: *Why not slide down the Cannonball Chute on your next birthday?* 'But I thought everybody got those … you know … the hard sell. Are you telling me that you were somehow responsible?'

Rorgan Tyne nodded. '*I* put them in your letterbox — stole them, of course.'

'You mean they were meant just for *me*? To get me thinking about going to Aqua Mania for my birthday?' Garry stood up and looked through the small window towards his house. 'But how did you know I'd go there on my birthday? I mean, it was a bit of a long shot, wasn't it? I could have gone anywhere.'

'But it worked, didn't it? You played right into my hands, Garry Tenon.'

'And if I hadn't?'

'Just would have tried something else.'

'But why didn't you just come to Port Vlamingh and stay? Why did you have to swap places?'

Rorgan Tyne sighed impatiently. 'Really Garry. For an intelligent boy you are *so* dim!'

Garry was speechless. Dim! Who was the dim one here? This kid must be the biggest idiot he'd ever met. Going to all that trouble to run away from a few measly problems. But then he stopped himself — on the other hand, Rorgan Tyne *wasn't* stupid. He seemed to be very, very clever. Garry said nothing. He had to start being careful.

'Because, as Rorgan Tyne,' continued the boy, annoyed that Garry hadn't reacted to his remark, 'I don't really exist here, do I? I don't have a birth certificate or a family or anything to prove that I'm a citizen. I wouldn't be able to go to school or get a job. I *had* to change identities.'

'So the mat ...'

'Ah, the mat. I was wondering when that would come up.' He rocked rhythmically. 'I had a teacher called ...'

'Master.'

Rorgan Tyne's eyes widened. 'Very impressive, Garry. You *have* been doing your homework! No doubt that bossy Pree Stappa filled you in. Anyway, Master and I designed a computer disguised as a mat. It detects heat — only body heat — and changes it into energy. When you go down a slide like the Snake or the Cannonball Chute, the mat travels so fast that your body matter compacts and then breaks through the barrier into another dimension.'

'And when two people go down ...'

'Ah, now that's more exciting but it requires a highly developed abstract mind to understand it.'

Garry was not about to be intimidated. 'Try me,' he said.

'Well, in layman's terms, the computer tracks the person following and transmits ultrasonic frequencies through the conductible water. These waves bounce from one person to the other and as momentum increases, the molecular structures combine as the matter from each body compacts. For a brief moment this mass is one person and then it separates, resulting in two people who have changed bodies and worlds.'

'Wow! So is that the Beady Eyes Theory?'

Rorgan Tyne looked up quickly. 'How did you know that?' he snapped resentfully.

'Pree Stappa and the others mentioned it but they didn't know what it was.'

'Obviously,' said Rorgan Tyne, dryly.

'Why's it called Beady Eyes? I mean, I know snakes have beady eyes, but I don't understand why ...?' He broke off as Rorgan Tyne suddenly stopped rocking and let out a hoot of laughter. 'What's the matter? Be quiet. You'll wake up the whole neighbourhood,' warned Garry looking towards his house again.

'Not *beady eyes*, dummy,' Rorgan Tyne spluttered. 'B ... D ... I ... S. It's an acronym.'

'Oh,' said Garry feeling incredibly foolish. 'BDIS,' he spelled under his breath.

Rorgan Tyne sat on the edge of the chair, doubled over, laughing and clutching his stomach as though he had a severe pain. 'Beady eyes! Beady eyes!' he snorted.

Despite himself, Garry managed a smile. 'What does BDIS stand for?'

'Bi-Dimensional-Identity-Switch. It's when two people swap identities and dimensions using the mat.' Rorgan Tyne continued rocking, arms folded, a smug look on his face.

'So, you came here,' Garry said slowly, trying to make sense of the theory, 'on the mat by sliding down the Snake ...'

'Yes, and when I pushed you over at Aqua Mania I gave you the mat. Then you went down the Cannonball Chute and I was right behind. You became me and went to my world and I became you and stayed here in Port Vlamingh.'

'So if we rode the Cannonball Chute right now,

you on the mat and me following, our identities would switch back and you'd go to Lennox City and I'd stay here?'

'Yes,' said Rorgan Tyne, narrowing his eyes, 'but that's not going to happen.'

'And I'd have to *follow* you?'

'Yes. If we came into contact the ultrasonic transmission would drop to almost zero. Then we wouldn't switch bodies but we'd both go to Lennox City.'

'I'd still look like you?'

'Yes, but like I said, it's not going to happen.'

'You reckon you got what you wanted?' Garry said carefully.

Rorgan Tyne smirked. 'Well, you could say that.'

'Except you haven't really, have you?'

'What do you mean?' replied Rorgan Tyne sharply. He started to rock more vigorously.

'Your plan hasn't worked. You didn't reckon I'd figure out how to get back to Port Vlamingh, did you? You thought you'd be able to escape all your problems coming here but they've only just begun. That's why you're running away again.'

'You're wrong, Garry Tenon.'

'Oh come on! What about the police I saw tonight. In trouble already, Rorgan Tyne?'

'Just borrowed a few things from the shop ...'

'Shoplifting huh? And my parents. They would've noticed a big change in their son's behaviour. You've been grounded, haven't you?'

Rorgan Tyne rocked harder, staring at Garry, silent.

'And what about Cameron and my other friends?' Garry continued. He was guessing now but he had a feeling that he was right. 'Fallen out with them, too? How was school today? Bet you wagged it.'

Rorgan Tyne's face was like thunder. The rocking chair groaned under his weight.

'Thought so. And now you're running away again.'

Rorgan Tyne's smug look had vanished.

'With the Link,' said Garry, pointing to the leather watchstrap.

'How did you know about that?'

'So you did steal it!'

'Sure, it was a cinch. I'd been to the Pivot with Master and it didn't take long to work out how it operated.'

Garry listened to the boy's boasts of eluding the central security system with a homemade bogus DNA identification print, and then temporarily sabotaging power and video surveillance using his voice-activated mini computer. 'I'd reprogrammed it with data from the Pivot's computer databank,' he explained casually. 'Everything shut down for about five minutes giving me time to take the Link and get out.'

'But why did you do it?' asked Garry, grappling with the mind-boggling brilliance of the boy's technological wizardry and the sheer idiocy of causing mass destruction.

Rorgan Tyne shrugged again but shifted uneasily in the chair. 'Just wanted to get back at them all, I suppose.'

'But didn't you realise the consequences? Do you have any idea what's happened to Lennox City now the Link's gone?'

'I suppose they're having problems with the weather.'

'Problems! You can say that again. The place is a total disaster!'

'What do you mean?' His darting eyes betrayed sudden alarm.

'You just happen to have stolen a critical component of the Modulator, that's what I mean. The weather's gone completely berserk. One minute there are severe storms, then it's boiling hot, then it snows. Animals and crops are going to die and food's already a priority. Everybody's been evacuated to the subcaves while they look for the Link. Trouble is, they won't find you in Lennox City and the supplies in the subcaves can't last forever.' Garry stopped. Rorgan Tyne's jaw had dropped, his eyes wide in alarm. 'Wait a minute! You didn't know that would happen when you stole the Link, did you?'

'No ... I mean ... I thought it would just inconvenience everyone ... you know ... and then they'd replace the Link and everything would be all right.'

'It's an ancient rock that can't be replaced. But you could give it back and save Lennox City. It's not too late. We'll ride the Cannonball Chute. You'll have the mat and we'll be ourselves again and in our own dimensions.'

'But I can't go back! They'll know I stole it. *You* go,' said Rorgan Tyne desperately.

'What! No thanks! This is my home and I'm staying. You have to go.'

'I'm *not* going back!' cried Rorgan Tyne. He was really agitated now. He rocked back and forth at an alarming pace, the chair complaining loudly.

'Look out!' yelled Garry. 'You're going too high ... it'll break ...'

SNAP! The rotting wood collapsed and the chair sprang backwards, flinging Rorgan Tyne awkwardly into the air. His head hit the cement floor with a ghastly thud and he lay still.

16

Garry couldn't move. He stared at the boy on the floor then through the shed window to the house. He expected lights to come on, his father to come out with a torch. Surely they'd heard the noise? The seconds dragged on and there were no lights, no sounds except the loud thumping of his own heart.

He forced himself to look at Rorgan Tyne. The moonlight shone eerily on the boy's face. The face that was really Garry's. Was Rorgan Tyne unconscious? Was he dead? Playing dead? He crept up to the motionless figure. Would Rorgan Tyne suddenly jump up, grab him, force him into a chair and tie him up? That's what happened in *Night Terrors*, that creepy film he'd seen a couple of weeks ago. He wished he hadn't watched it now.

Rorgan Tyne moved slightly, groaned and went limp again. Not dead, then. Garry waited. Nothing happened. Slowly he reached across and touched Rorgan Tyne's head. It was strange, handling his own head. No blood. Good. Just a whopping lump. Definitely unconscious. What now? Snippets of *Night Terrors* danced in his brain.

Even before he saw the length of rope that always hung behind the door, Garry knew what he had to do. Quick! He had to hurry before Rorgan Tyne woke up. Where was the go-cart, though? He needed the cart. Desperately, he scanned the moonlit shed. In the corner. Yes.

He and Cameron had made the box go-cart weeks ago and had hitched it to Garry's bike. They'd ridden up and down the road, taking it in turns to sit in the box. It was fantastic! Even when Cameron had fallen out and gashed his nose. Blood everywhere. Six stitches. Unfortunately, after the accident the go-cart had become a 'no-cart'. But it was about to be resurrected.

Trying not to make a noise, Garry dragged the limp body into the box go-cart. He tied his captive's hands to the sides of the cart and cut the rope with the pocketknife he'd taken from Rorgan Tyne's room. Then he bound the boy's feet and pulled the cart through the door of the shed and down the grass to the side of the house where he'd hidden the mat. He shoved the mat in behind Rorgan Tyne's back and, pulling the cart behind him, set off for Cameron's place. His own bike was locked in the garage but Cameron's was still leaning up against the house where he'd left it earlier. Good old Cameron! He'd been able to help after all.

He attached the go-cart to the back of the bike and set off down the road in the direction of Aqua Mania. The cart bounced at every bump in the road and at one point nearly tipped over. But Garry pedalled on and on through the evening until finally he reached the Aqua Mania car park. He was exhausted and hungry and his legs ached but he was also elated. He'd won! First thing tomorrow when Aqua Mania opened he'd send Rorgan Tyne down the Cannonball Chute on the mat back to his world. He'd follow him down the water slide and their identities would switch back.

Easy.

Of course he didn't have the entrance money for Aqua Mania but he'd think of a way to get in — tomorrow.

Garry leaned the bike against a shed and slid exhausted to the ground. He looked at Rorgan Tyne, still unconscious. Boy, was he glad to be getting rid of him. What a jerk! Nothing but trouble. He rubbed his eyes, fighting sleep. He had to be awake when Rorgan Tyne regained consciousness. Besides, there was something he longed to see: leaning forward, he unclasped the watch covering from Rorgan Tyne's wrist and took out the Link.

It was indeed the shape of a link you would find in a large chain, not very heavy and made of a hard, transparent material. Spurts of white fire like miniature comets zoomed around inside it, reminding Garry of the lightning rebounding off the shell that covered Lennox City. Occasionally, the lights collided causing a brilliant explosion of colour. It was hard to imagine that such a small object held so much power and that its absence could cause such chaos and misery.

Garry closed his fingers over its smooth surface and considered his predicament. Somehow he had to convince Rorgan Tyne to save Lennox City but it was obvious the boy was scared. Scared enough to escape or do something silly like destroy the Link or even the mat. At least if Garry had them he could return the Link and get back to Port Vlamingh. But then he'd be wearing Rorgan Tyne's skin forever! He shook his tired head. No way. He wanted Lennox City to survive but he also yearned to be himself again. He could have both these things as long as Rorgan Tyne had the mat and wore the Link and went down the slide with him following. He would *push* him down if he had to.

With great care he replaced the Link in its hiding

place on Rorgan Tyne's wrist and secured the ropes around the boy's arms and feet. He leaned against the shed, determined to stay awake, but his eyes closed and his mind wandered ... and it wasn't long before it shut down.

In a moment he was asleep.

The jangling of keys woke him and he shivered in the freshness of the morning. Remembering his mission, Garry sat up with a start and peered around the corner of the shed. A man was opening the gates to Aqua Mania.

'What's happened? What's this place?' moaned a voice behind him. Rorgan Tyne was awake, squinting into the sunlight. 'Who tied my hands? Ooh!' he winced. 'My head!'

'You knocked yourself out last night when you fell off the rocking chair. I tied you up and brought you here in the go-cart.'

'Why? Where are we?' asked Rorgan Tyne, looking around. 'Ouch! My head hurts.'

'We're at Aqua Mania. You're going home and I'm going to be me again.'

Rorgan Tyne shifted uncomfortably in the cart. 'Can you untie me?'

'No way. You'll make a run for it.'

'No, I won't. Honest. I'm numb. I've got to walk around a bit. Anyway, you'll have to untie me sooner or later.'

'Okay, but no funny business,' said Garry, cutting the ropes with the pocket knife. Rorgan Tyne pulled himself out of the cart and rubbed the back of his head. He walked away unsteadily.

'Hey, no you don't!' cried Garry, expecting the boy to break out into a run.

'Geez,' said Rorgan Tyne, rubbing his head. 'I couldn't run if I wanted to. I'm going into Aqua Mania with you. Down the Cannonball Chute. Isn't that what you want? Trust me. Don't forget the mat.' And he walked towards the gate.

Trust him? He had to be joking!

'Last night,' Garry called, 'you said you'd never go back.' He picked up the mat and hurried to catch up.

'Did I? Well, I've changed my mind.'

'Why?'

'You're right. I should go back, fix up the mess I've made, own up. Anyway, I've had enough of your world.' He sniffed and shrugged his shoulders. 'I can see I'm not appreciated here.'

Garry fumed but kept quiet. Better not upset him now. It was too risky. What if he changed his mind again and ran off? What a nerd! Maybe if he stopped blaming everyone else for his troubles more people would 'appreciate' him. Still, he thought, at least he was going back. He wondered what had changed his mind. Maybe the bump on his head had made him see sense. Maybe he had concussion. But Garry had the feeling there was something more going on here … something not quite right … Rorgan Tyne was somehow different … he was up to something. Better be careful.

'Here we are,' whispered Rorgan Tyne, stopping at a telephone booth outside the entrance to Aqua Mania. The two boys watched the attendant behind a glass window at the gate about twenty metres away.

'Right, we'll make a run for it when her back's turned,' said Garry. 'Don't know about you but I certainly can't pay to get in.'

Rorgan Tyne rummaged in his pockets and produced some coins. 'This will do,' he said, smiling.

Garry looked at the coins. '*That's* not enough.'

'Isn't it? Watch and learn, Garry Tenon. Stay near the entrance but don't let *her* see you,' he said and pointed to the attendant.

Garry stared in bewilderment as Rorgan Tyne stepped into the phone booth, put the coins in the slot and punched some numbers. The woman attendant turned and disappeared behind a screen. Rorgan Tyne darted out of the phone box, grabbed Garry's arm and pulled him through the gates and behind a bush inside the water park fence line.

Garry's heart pumped like it would burst. They watched the attendant appear at the window again. She shook her head crossly.

'See?' said Rorgan Tyne. 'Easy. Done it before.'

'You rang *her*?' whispered Garry.

'Yes.'

'And the phone's behind that screen?'

'Right again. Clever, huh?'

Garry looked at the boy beside him. Clever? No … devious. He had to watch him. 'How did you know *she'd* answer, though? I mean what if there'd been someone else there?'

'Never is right on opening time. Come on.'

Casually, Rorgan Tyne strolled out from the bush and walked towards the Cannonball Chute. Garry followed. He half expected to be caught but as the minutes passed and nothing happened, he began to relax.

Rorgan Tyne quickened his pace but Garry, feeling the load of the mat, had trouble keeping up. Why was he going so fast? Why the hurry? An uneasy feeling churned in his gut. There was something wrong about all of this.

At the base of the steps leading up to the giant water slide, Rorgan Tyne paused to collect an Aqua Mania mat.

'Here,' he said, holding out the mat for Garry to take. 'Give me my mat.'

Garry hesitated.

'Come on. I can't go home without my mat. Look, you're getting what you wanted. Follow me down the slide and you'll be Garry Tenon again. Look, I really want to go home, too. Trust me.'

There it was again. *Trust me.* Could he trust this boy who had already deceived him? Of course he couldn't, but he had to give him the mat. There was no other way to wear his own skin again.

The second they exchanged mats Garry regretted it. Rorgan Tyne smirked nastily, turned and fled up the steps towards the summit of the Cannonball Chute.

'You're a fool,' he yelled over his shoulder.

Garry tore after him, swearing furiously under his breath. Why had he let the mat go so easily? What was this boy up to?

He reached the top and saw Rorgan Tyne standing at the entrance to the slide. 'What took you so long?' he asked as Garry stumbled into view.

Breathing hard, Garry stared at his antagonist. Stay calm. Don't panic. Don't let him fool you again.

'I'm surprised you didn't catch onto my plan,' taunted Rorgan Tyne.

'What plan?' said Garry, throwing his mat onto the platform.

'You're so stupid, Garry. Do you think that once I'm back in Lennox City I'll really own up?'

'Well maybe not. But you'll return the Link, won't you? I mean you won't be able to live there if you don't. Pree Stappa can help you.'

'Ha! Pree Stappa!' he snorted.

'What about Mother? She really seems to like you, and perhaps Lado Kaan ...'

'No way! Are you crazy? Do you know what he'd do?'

Garry looked at the desperate eyes and turned-down mouth. 'You know, I thought you were just angry but you're really scared, aren't you?'

'Oh sure. I'm scared and the moon's made of cheese,' said Rorgan Tyne tossing back his head. 'Being scared isn't part of my plan.' But there was a distinct tremor in his voice.

'So what is your plan?'

'You want your identity back? You're welcome to it. Just slide down after me. I'll come straight back from Lennox City though and find some other unsuspecting kid — maybe Regan Norty.'

'But what about the Link?' Garry felt the panic rising in his throat.

This time Rorgan Tyne's voice shook with unmistakable fear. 'I can't take it. They'll probably all be waiting for me.'

'No they won't,' Garry protested. 'I asked Pree Stappa not to say anything until ...'

'I told you. I can't take it!' cried Rorgan Tyne, tearing off the leather wrist strap and throwing it down.

'You've got to!' screamed Garry as he scrambled towards the entrance of the tunnel where the leather strap lay. His fingers grasped the strap just as Rorgan Tyne turned to slide down the Cannonball Chute on the mat.

'Nooooo!' yelled Garry, flinging himself into the tunnel. Waves of water gushed over his face as he flew down. He felt disorientated and sick because of the water he'd swallowed but his mind was bursting with triumph: while his left hand held the watchstrap containing the Link, with his right hand he had a firm grip on one of Rorgan Tyne's ankles.

'Let go, you idiot!' Rorgan Tyne's voice boomed through the dark tunnel. He thrashed his feet, trying to shake Garry off.

But Garry clung on tightly to both the Link and the ankle. Pain shot through his hand but he told himself over and over that he mustn't let go. He couldn't let Rorgan Tyne get away with this. If he let go now he'd remain in Port Vlamingh with the Link and he'd never be able to return it without the mat. Lennox City and Pree Stappa and the others would die! Faster and faster they whizzed down the slide and Garry closed his eyes and concentrated. Hang on!

'Get off!' screamed Rorgan Tyne and he tugged his leg vigorously.

Garry's fingers slipped. He slammed into the wall of the tunnel, losing his forward momentum, while only metres ahead of him Rorgan Tyne and the mat careered through the slide exit.

'Ahhhh!' came an astonished cry.

There was a whiplike crack and then silence.

Dizzily, Garry lifted his head from the icy surface of the Snake. For a moment he was confused and was only aware of an ache in his hand. He flexed his fingers and closed his eyes while he tried to regain his breath. A noise that was like the pitiful bleating of a lamb echoed from below. Creeping cautiously and unsteadily towards the tunnel exit, he peered over the edge, shivering. He had made it back to Lennox City!

'Ow ... ow,' groaned Rorgan Tyne far below. 'Somebody help me.'

Through the falling snow, Garry saw the boy who wore his face lying on the mat on a large slab of ice, a great crack extending beyond him to the edge of the frozen pool. Garry fingered the scar on his chin. He desperately wanted to be home in his own body but the switch could only happen when both he and Rorgan Tyne had ridden the Snake again, Garry on the mat. First he must return the Link.

'My legs! I can't move!'

But even as Rorgan Tyne shouted the snow stopped falling, a searing heat bore down and in seconds the ice was melting. Rorgan Tyne slid from the mat, thrashing his arms around in the water, his legs powerless.

'Help me,' he gasped, swallowing water. He coughed violently and sank, unable to tread water. Rorgan Tyne was drowning.

Garry watched, horrified. He couldn't let a person drown, not even a troublemaker like Rorgan Tyne, who, he suspected, might not be so helpful if it were him, Garry, in difficulty. But the water was so far down. He couldn't jump. His tired mind was a jumble. What should he do? His left fist closed tighter on the Link.

'Help!' Garry yelled. 'Somebody, help!'

But there was nobody. Only him.

Desperately, he looked at the sinking figure and his mind was suddenly alert. What if Rorgan Tyne *did* drown? Could you switch places with a dead person? Probably not. That did it. He jumped.

The water was warm on the surface but freezing underneath. Frantically, he searched for Rorgan Tyne. Again and again he dived but he couldn't find him. He was tiring, his brain numb. And then all determination left him and he felt his mind drifting. The water was pleasantly warm, even hot, like a bubbling spa. Now it was he who was sinking and he didn't care.

'Garry!' called a familiar voice. 'I'm here!' And strong hands grasped him and pulled him from the water.

'The mat, the mat,' he heard himself cry. 'Don't forget the mat.'

He strained to open his eyes but all energy had left him. He was dimly aware of being carried to a cool place and sinking to the ground, breathing so hard he thought his insides would burst.

'The mat … hide it … don't let him …' mumbled Garry. Forcing his eyes open at last he saw Pree Stappa leaning over him, fingering the silver chain around his neck.

'You made it,' she whispered.

'Pree Stappa … take this!' And he finally unclenched his left fist just as he lost consciousness.

Garry turned on his side and slowly opened his eyes. He was lying on Rorgan Tyne's bed, in clean, dry clothes, a warm sun streaming through the window. Mother sat next to the bed, smiling at him. She leaned forward as he stirred.

'Ohh,' he murmured groggily. 'What happened?' He sat up too quickly and immediately sank back into the pillows.

'Careful, Rorgan Tyne,' said Mother, stroking his forehead. 'Lie still for a minute. We nearly lost you, you know. The doctor said you probably hadn't eaten for a while and you were so weak you nearly drowned. Are you hungry?'

'Yes.'

'I'll send Pree Stappa up with something. She saved you, you know, and the other boy. The police are talking to him right now. I don't know why on earth he stole the Link.' Mother started towards the door then turned back and smiled. 'You're a hero. You've

103

saved Lennox City. I always knew you'd come good.'

Before Garry could say anything, she'd gone.

He closed his eyes, a barrage of questions bombarding his cloudy brain. Where was Rorgan Tyne and what had he told the police? Had Pree Stappa hidden the mat? Well, at least she was still here and he *had* saved Lennox City.

The bedroom door opened, startling him, and Pree Stappa darted in balancing a tray in one hand. She closed the door and hurried towards him. 'You did it!' she beamed, pointing to the perfect day through the window.

'Hey,' he said, slowly sitting up. 'How come you're still here? Wasn't your mum picking you up?'

'By the time she arrived it was too late and too dangerous to go home. So we spent the night here. She's gone back but I insisted on staying. There's something I have to tell you ...'

'I'm glad you stayed. I nearly drowned, I know ... thank you ... for saving me.'

'Just happy you came back,' she smiled, freckles stretching across her nose. 'Hungry?'

'Am I ever.' He demolished a sandwich to prove it and took another.

'Listen,' she said, sitting down on the chair next to the bed. 'There isn't much time. I just overheard Mother talking to the police. They'll be here in a minute wanting to question you about the Link. They've just been with Rorgan Tyne. Well, they don't realise he's Rorgan Tyne, of course.'

'Where is he? Is he all right?'

'He's in Drey Allenbow's room. His legs are severely bruised. It's a miracle they aren't broken. Apparently he can only just hobble.'

'Do you know what he told the police?'

'Yes. He said *you* stole the Link and he was trying to get it from you when you both fell from the Snake. He's actually put the blame on *himself*. Why would he do that?'

Garry scratched the scar on his chin. 'I think he's still planning on getting out of here. I bet he's already looking for the mat, so he can slide down the Snake and leave forever.'

'And you'd be stuck with the blame.'

'And stuck in Rorgan Tyne's itchy skin.' Garry made a face.

'What are we going to do?'

Garry struggled with a glimmer of an idea in the back of his mind. He shut his eyes and concentrated and suddenly a hot stab of excitement hit his stomach. It was the feeling he got when he worked something out for himself. Like getting the hang of a new computer game. 'You've hidden the mat, haven't you?'

'Yes, I locked it in the storeroom.' She pulled out the key from around her neck. 'Why's the mat so important?'

Garry finished his third sandwich. His strength was returning and he was thinking fast. 'It's not an ordinary mat. You need it to change worlds and identities, but I'll explain later.'

'Shh!' Pree Stappa warned and they both listened. Footsteps and voices were coming along the corridor. 'This is it. Your turn for interrogation. What are you going to tell them?'

'That I stole the Link but decided to return and save Lennox City,' he beamed.

'What? Are you mad?'

'Can't explain now,' he whispered urgently as the voices came nearer. 'After I've spoken to the police I'll get away somehow. Meet me in the Snake's storeroom. Then I'll …'

The door opened. Pree Stappa stood up quickly and Garry stuffed the last of his sandwich into his mouth.

'I'll leave you to it,' said Pree Stappa, grabbing the tray and gliding through the open door past Mother and the police officer. She nearly bumped into Lado Kaan wheeling himself into the room. Blue veins, bulging with anger, patterned his neck like swollen tidal rivers.

'Rorgan Tyne! What the hell's going on!' bellowed Lado Kaan.

Garry's insides jumped.

'I think,' said the police officer, calmly ignoring the outburst, 'you might be able to help us with our inquiries, Rorgan Tyne.'

Garry sat up in bed. He looked at Lado Kaan and the tall uniformed policeman, and Mother, her face puzzled and sad. He wanted to hug her and tell her he hadn't stolen the Link. He had to maintain Rorgan Tyne's cool arrogance and yet sound remorseful and his whole body ached with fear. 'It's simple,' he said at last. 'I took the Link. But when I saw what was happening to Lennox City,' he added, looking at Mother, 'I brought it back.'

20

'... so that's how I did it and why I decided to return the Link. Unfortunately, that annoying blond-haired kid didn't seem to believe me when I said I was on my way to the Pivot.'

Garry held his head high and looked from one face to another, assuming an expression which he hoped conveyed remorse but a hint of Rorgan Tyne's defiance. He'd been careful to include an explanation of how the Link was stolen and was thankful that he'd listened attentively to Rorgan Tyne's boasts. He'd kept his story simple — had said nothing about the BDIS theory or the mat — and hoped like hell that it sounded plausible.

'This other boy,' said the police officer, 'How do you know him?'

Garry shrugged. 'I've only just met him.'

'He says he convinced you to return the Link.'

Garry shrugged. 'I'd decided to even before he suggested it.'

The police officer scribbled in a little book for several minutes. Lado Kaan was silent, reproachful, reminding Garry of the way his own parents had looked the last time he'd seen them. Mother's face had softened.

Finally Lado Kaan spoke. 'Do you think,' he said, looking at the police officer and Mother, 'that I could have a few moments with my son — alone?' It was more of a command than a request.

'Yes, of course,' said the policeman, 'but I must remind you that …'

'I want to speak to my son,' said Lado Kaan, his voice low and threatening.

The officer seemed to be used to dealing with difficult people. He consulted his watch. 'We'll be back in five minutes,' he said, standing at the door with Mother.

The door closed and there was silence. Garry gulped. What would this man say? Do?

'What do you think you're playing at!' Lado Kaan exploded at last. 'Why?'

Garry jumped. 'I … I …' he faltered.

'You're a disgrace, Rorgan Tyne, you know that? Everything I've done for you and this is the way you repay me! Given you opportunities, sent you to this exclusive diving school, and this is what I get! You might have returned the Link but what you haven't

109

explained is why the hell you stole it in the first place.'

Garry froze. Even though he hadn't done anything wrong, he felt a stab of horror. His own father had never spoken to him like this. What was it Rorgan Tyne had said? *You obviously haven't met my father*. Well now that he had, Garry finally understood Rorgan Tyne's fear.

Lado Kaan's voice became louder and his face redder as he ranted on and on, all the time pushing his wheelchair around the room.

'I've got you out of scrapes before but this time, my boy, you're on your own. Stealing the Link ... what do you think ...'

'But I brought the Link back!' protested Garry.

'That's beside the point. You stole it!'

'Why are you such an angry old man?' Garry blurted out, surprising himself as well as Lado Kaan.

The man stopped shouting and the veins in his neck looked as though they'd rupture at any moment. 'Because, if you hadn't noticed, I'm stuck in this wheelchair for the rest of my life,' he whispered.

'Then stop blaming it on me,' said Garry. 'You make my life hell!'

There was shocked silence.

Suddenly Lado Kaan's face crumpled as though

he were in pain. He pushed his fists into his chest. 'My heart, my heart!'

'What's the matter?' Garry asked, rushing forwards.

The man shoved him away. 'What's it to you? You don't really care. How did you become so selfish?' he gasped, too theatrically.

Garry wasn't fooled by the man's feigned performance. 'I learnt it,' he answered quietly, 'from you.'

Lado Kaan winced and couldn't have looked more hurt if Garry had slapped him across the face. He clutched his heart again. 'I care about you, my boy ... I know I haven't been the perfect father ... let's talk ...'

Garry wanted to stay but saw the opportunity to escape and was already at the door.

'Mother, anyone! Help! Lado Kaan ... I think he's having a heart attack!'

He only stayed a moment while Mother and the police officer attended to Lado Kaan. And then, while no one was looking, he quietly slipped away.

21

Pree Stappa was waiting for him when he charged into the storeroom.

'I was beginning to wonder if you'd ever get here,' she whispered. 'How'd you escape? I thought maybe I should have created a diversion like set fire to the house or something.' Freckles danced across her nose as she smiled.

Garry sank into the pile of mats, catching his breath, adrenaline pumping.

'Hey, what's up?' she said. 'What's happened?'

'Lado Kaan …'

'What's he done now?'

Garry frowned and related the story of his police interview and Lado Kaan's outburst.

'Good for you,' she said. 'I don't think Rorgan Tyne's ever stood up to him before. That'll give him something to think about. Could be a new beginning for both of them.'

'Do you think he faked an attack so I could escape?'

'Maybe. Or it could have been to win your sympathy. He's a bit of a manipulator, if you hadn't already noticed. He works himself into a frenzy and plays on the attention it brings him. Don't worry. He'll be all right. Now, what is it with this mat? What does it do?'

Garry glanced at his watch. It wouldn't be long before they came looking for him. 'Remember when I went down the Snake looking for a secret tunnel?' he asked.

'Yes, what happened? Did you find it?'

He quickly explained how he'd discovered the importance of the mat and how he'd travelled back to his home and found Rorgan Tyne in the process of ruining his life. He described his meeting with him and told her why Rorgan Tyne had used the BDIS Theory to escape from Lennox City.

'And we thought it was beady eyes,' giggled Pree Stappa. 'The Snake's beady eyes, Rorgan Tyne's black beady eyes. It was just coincidence?'

Garry laughed. 'I felt pretty stupid, I can tell you.'

'So you got him to Aqua Mania on the go-cart and then what?'

He told her the rest of the story, finishing with Rorgan Tyne's attempt to trick him and avoid returning the Link.

'You know, I think he really needs help,' said Pree

Stappa. 'He's exceptionally clever — a genius maybe, if the mat was basically his idea — but he's also very strange.'

'You mean like a mad professor?'

She smiled. 'Well, not mad, but a bit screwed up. Kids our age don't usually act like him. He's sort of angry all the time, don't you think? Maybe he should talk to someone.'

'Well, I reckon Lado Kaan will finally come to his senses and help him, and you can put in a good word for him, too. Tell the police he didn't realise that stealing the Link would be so catastrophic. And the scene's set for him to make a new start — he's prepared to take the blame for stealing the Link as well as the credit for its return. All we have to do now is use the BDIS Theory and switch places.'

She looked at him with admiration. 'Nice work, but how will we do that? Rorgan Tyne will never agree.'

He waved an impatient hand at her, eager to get on with the plan. 'No, of course he won't so that's why we've got to lure him here. Leave the mat in the corner against the wall and go and see him.'

'What?'

'We have to let him believe he's outwitted us.'

'But what if I can't see him?'

'You'll find a way, I know.'

'And what do I tell him?'

'Just be really cool and let him know where the mat is — he'll ask for sure. Pretend you don't know why it's so significant. Man oh man! I bet he'll be hobbling over here as fast as he can.'

'But what if he can't get away?'

'He's Rorgan Tyne. He'll find a way. Don't say anything about my confession, though. It'll make him suspicious. Say that they're holding me for questioning and you haven't been able to talk with me. He'll be ecstatic his plan's working. Just hope nobody's told him I'm already missing or what I said to the police.' He glanced anxiously at his watch again, crept to the door of the storeroom and peered out. There was no one there.

'But you won't let him go down the Snake on the mat. Right?' whispered Pree Stappa, following him to the door.

'Right. I'll be waiting for him at the entrance. If I can't convince him to switch places we'll have to push him down. When I give a signal, come up behind and distract him — jump on him or something. I'll snatch the mat, then go down the Snake. You'll have to push him down behind me. With weak legs he's not going to be able to fight back much.'

'How close to you does he have to be?'

'Right behind me I think. But don't push too soon.

If he touches me or the mat the ultrasonic transmission is too weak for the identity switch to work. We need to hurry before he realises what's going on. Are you ready?'

'Yes.' She turned to go but hesitated. 'Garry, you'll have the mat when you return to Port Vlamingh. Will you come back do you think?'

'What, here to Lennox City?'

'Yes … the Diving Championship's in a couple of months … perhaps you could … I mean you're the only one who can do a triple twist torpedo.'

Garry laughed. 'But that was a *fluke*, remember?'

'Yes, but you could do it again.'

'Maybe … I might come back.'

There was silence. Garry looked at his feet. He suddenly felt awkward and hot and he couldn't think of anything else to say.

'I'd better get going. See you,' Pree Stappa said finally and set off, jogging across the pavement. He watched her disappear into the house, his face still burning with embarrassment. Then he turned and sprinted up the steps to the top of the slide.

It was late afternoon and he crouched by the railings keeping watch on the house. As he expected, the police came looking for him but miraculously didn't check the Snake. The minutes dragged on, the shadows became longer and the lights of the city came on. But there was no sign of Rorgan Tyne. Garry waited nervously. What if he hadn't taken the bait? What if Pree Stappa hadn't been able to talk to him? What if he knew about the confession? And just when the worry was turning to panic, he saw a figure.

It was Rorgan Tyne. He was on crutches and he was in a hurry. He pulled the reluctant kelpie along at the end of a short rope. Both boy and dog disappeared into the shadows and Garry waited, knowing that Rorgan Tyne was looking for the mat. Minutes went by. Where was he? Surely he wouldn't tackle the steps on crutches? Suddenly there was a soft hissing and gurgling. Of course! Rorgan Tyne had turned on the water pump. He reappeared, stopped at the lift entrance, pushed the button and stepped into the lift.

Garry's heart thumped. This was it. Be careful, be careful. He crept in front of the tunnel, ready to stand up. He heard the click of the lift as it reached its destination. The doors opened and Rorgan Tyne adjusted the mat and shuffled out into the fading light. The dog whined and stood its ground. The boy tugged on the rope and tried to swipe the dog with a crutch.

Garry stood up, hands on hips, legs astride, guarding the entrance to the Snake.

'What took you so long?' he asked.

22

Rorgan Tyne staggered backwards in surprise.

'What the ...?' he gasped.

'Going somewhere?' asked Garry calmly, though he felt sick with fear. 'In my skin? Leaving me to be Rorgan Tyne forever?'

Rorgan Tyne regained his composure. 'Clever, huh?' he said. But Garry saw the terror in his eyes.

'Yes, it was, actually,' said Garry, 'but I can't let you do it, Rorgan Tyne.'

'No? I have the mat, remember?'

'Yes, thanks to Pree Stappa.'

Rorgan Tyne looked confused. 'I asked her where it was ... she told me ... I couldn't believe my luck ... she said she couldn't understand what I'd want with a dirty old mat but I was welcome to it if I wanted it.' He paused, as though mentally piecing together a jigsaw. Shrugging, he looked up at Garry, narrowing his eyes. 'She said the police believed my story ... that you were being held for questioning … but you're here … how did you …?'

'I lied. I'm sorry it had to be like this,' said a voice behind Rorgan Tyne. He swung around to face Pree Stappa who had come up the stairs. 'We knew you'd be looking for the mat so I just helped you along a bit. Rorgan Tyne, you've got to switch places with Garry. He shouldn't take the consequences of something he didn't do. You can't leave him here without any way of getting home.'

As she spoke, she moved towards him. He flung the rope and crutches to one side and hugged the mat to his chest. The kelpie, free at last, bounded towards Garry and sat at his feet.

'You're not having the mat. You're not ruining my plan,' Rorgan Tyne said menacingly.

'It was a good plan,' said Garry, trying to keep calm. 'So I decided to use it, too.'

'What do you mean?'

'Well, I knew what you had in mind when I heard you'd blamed me for stealing the Link. I certainly didn't want to be Rorgan Tyne for the rest of my life, especially since I'd been accused of stealing. So I confessed so that when we switched places, there'd be no doubt that Rorgan Tyne did it. But I think I've convinced the police of something else. Something that will help you.'

'What do you mean?'

'I told them I was returning the Link to the Pivot.'

'So?'

Garry was surprised. 'Don't you get it? You're a hero! You've been given the credit for saving Lennox City.'

'You think you're so clever, Garry Tenon. I didn't ask for your help. I still have the mat and I'm not switching places.' He clicked his fingers at the kelpie. 'Come here, dog!' he commanded but the animal didn't move.

'I spoke to your father too,' said Garry sensing his plan about to fall in a heap.

Rorgan Tyne's eyes flashed with fear. 'What did he want?'

'I basically told him he was an angry selfish old man. I think he actually listened. He said …'

Rorgan Tyne turned on him. 'What! Are you crazy? He'll kill me!'

'So you *are* going back?'

'Stop twisting my words, Mr Wise Guy. You don't know what you've done. You're going to cop it now.'

'I don't think so,' said Pree Stappa. 'By standing up to him, Garry gave Lado Kaan something to think about other than himself. I know that once you switch identities things will be …'

'Lies! Lies! It's just another trick.'

'You didn't mean to cause so much damage when

you stole the Link, did you?' Pree Stappa persisted, still moving forward, her voice soft. 'And I know you really wanted to return the Link. Lado Kaan and Mother realise that, too. We all want to help you.'

'Help me! You hate me! You all hate me! You want me to own up ... take the blame ... my father will ...' And he looked desperately at Garry who still blocked the entrance to the Snake.

'I don't hate you ...'

'Save your breath, Pree Stappa,' warned Rorgan Tyne. 'You!' He looked at Garry. 'Get out of my way. And you too, traitor,' he said to the dog.

The dog whined and Garry stroked its head.

'Please, Rorgan Tyne,' begged Pree Stappa. 'Let Garry have the mat. You can't keep running. You need help. I'll tell them ...'

'Shut up! I don't want your help,' Rorgan Tyne yelled at her. Clutching the mat firmly to his chest, he turned his back on her and limped towards the Snake's entrance.

Garry stood his ground. Every hair on his body bristled with anticipation. 'Grab him!' he yelled.

Pree Stappa and the dog sprang towards Rorgan Tyne. Garry dived forward but despite his damaged legs, Rorgan Tyne managed to twist free, flinging Pree Stappa into the tunnel's entrance. She desperately tried to heave herself out of the Snake, her fingers clasping the side of the transparent tube, but the water was sucking her down.

It was all going wrong. It wasn't happening the way Garry had intended. Rorgan Tyne was at the entrance now, kicking at the dog as it tried to bite him. Garry struggled to his feet. Fear inside him ticked away like an unexploded bomb. He couldn't let Rorgan Tyne win! Not now. Not after everything that had happened. He wanted to go home, to be himself. He wanted everything to be normal again. Suddenly, the ticking stopped and the bomb inside him exploded.

'Aaargh!' he yelled, lunging himself at Rorgan Tyne and wrestling him to the ground.

Screaming with pain Rorgan Tyne writhed on his stomach and the dog seized the mat and dragged it away from the boy's searching fingers. Crouched on its haunches, it guarded its prize with bared teeth and eyed Rorgan Tyne as though he were an errant sheep.

'Good dog!' yelled Garry as he scrambled on all fours to the entrance and pulled Pree Stappa clear. Then with the kelpie dancing around them barking encouragement, they dragged the kicking Rorgan Tyne to the Snake.

'My legs! Ouch! Let me go!'

'Get the mat!' yelled Garry, backing towards the

entrance at the same time keeping an eye on Rorgan Tyne who had managed to stand up. 'I'm going down!'

Pree Stappa picked up the mat and hurled it over to him but he stepped back too far and slipped onto his stomach at the water's edge, the mat just out of his reach. In an instant, the kelpie sprang onto it and skidded forwards. Garry grasped it and plunged down the Snake feet first, arm around the prostrate dog. He just managed to catch a glimpse of a surprised Rorgan Tyne falling into the tunnel with help from Pree Stappa before darkness enveloped him.

They sped down, Garry's tears of relief mingling with the water as he and the dog hurtled faster and faster towards ... home.

Garry lay on his bed … *his* bed … fingering the chain around his neck and stroking the smooth hair of the kelpie beside him. When he'd returned a week ago he'd endured the full extent of his parents' seesawing emotions — hugging him one moment then chastising him the next for his wayward behaviour. He was grounded, of course, and the bedraggled dog was banned from the house.

Eager to make amends and confident in the knowledge that he was totally innocent, Garry accepted responsibility for Rorgan Tyne's conduct, and when they realised the old Garry was back, his parents' tough stand mellowed. They no longer spoke of counselling sessions and the dog was allowed to stay having proved he was homeless, house-trained and vermin free.

Garry sighed, relieved that everything was just about back to normal. But it would never be the same, he reminded himself. You don't live in another boy's body, squeeze through space on a computerised mat and save a city from destruction without your life changing forever — and for the better. After everything he'd been through, he knew he could take on any challenge life threw at him. And now that he thought about it, he had Rorgan Tyne to thank for that.

He wondered how the boy was coping in Lennox City. He hoped he'd accepted the credit for returning the Link and was putting his exceptional talents to good use. Lado Kaan would stand by him, Garry was certain of that. And so would Mother and Pree Stappa.

Pree Stappa. He frowned thoughtfully. What a girl! He really owed her, big time. If it hadn't been for her … well, he probably wouldn't be back in his skin, would he? And he hadn't even thanked her properly or said goodbye. And he still had her necklace.

A knock at the door startled him and he and the dog sat up.

'It's me, son,' called his dad.

'Come in.'

He poked his head around the door. 'Just wondered how you're going,' he said, walking across the room and sitting on his bed.

'Great,' Garry replied.

Dad smiled and stroked the kelpie's ears. 'You know what?' he said. 'It's good to have you back.' He looked approvingly around his room. 'Mm, glad to see you've tidied up. That other guy was a slob.'

Garry looked quizzically at his father's emotionless face then followed his gaze to the ceiling where a model plane hung. He glanced at his microscope, hockey stick, toy car collection and the stack of computer games on his desk. All of them were prized possessions but none would ever rival his most recent acquisition. It stood hidden at the back of his wardrobe and looked like an ordinary, black water slide mat.

Acknowledgements

I wish to thank Alex and Theo Gaunt whose expert knowledge of diving techniques and terminology was invaluable.

My thanks also to Janet Blagg for her perceptive editing and wise words, and to Marion Duke for the great cover.

First published 2003 by
FREMANTLE ARTS CENTRE PRESS
25 Quarry Street, Fremantle
(PO Box 158, North Fremantle 6159)
Western Australia.
www.facp.iinet.net.au

Consultant Editor Janet Blagg.
Production Coordinator Cate Sutherland.
Cover Designer Marion Duke.

Typeset by Fremantle Arts Centre Press
and printed by Griffin Press.

National Library of Australia
Cataloguing-in-publication data

Coghlan, Jo (Joanne), 1959– .
Switched.

For young adults.
ISBN 1 86368 350 X.

1. Identity (Psychology) — Fiction. I. Title.

A823.3.

The State of Western Australia has made an investment in this project
through ArtsWA in association with the Lotteries Commission.

Publication of this title was assisted by the Commonwealth Government
through the Australia Council, its arts funding and advisory body.